the MIGHTY QUINN

BY

ROBYN PARNELL

····

Illustrations by Katie and Aaron DeYoe

SCARLETTA JUNIOR READERS

MINNEAPOLIS, MINNESOTA

The Lexile Framework for Reading ® Lexile measure ® 700L

Illustrations: Katie and Aaron DeYoe
Design & Composition: Mighty Media, Inc., Minneapolis, Minnesota

Library of Congress Cataloging-in-Publication Data

Parnell, Robyn.
 The mighty Quinn / by Robyn Parnell ; illustrated by Aaron and Katie DeYoe.
  pages cm
 Summary: Fifth-graders Quinn and Neally solve a mystery, thwart a bully, and realize that the fabled ability to belch the entire alphabet might very possibly trump any award ever presented at Turner Creek School. Includes discussion questions and activities.
 ISBN 978-1-938063-10-7 (pbk. : alk. paper) -- ISBN 1-938063-10-4 (pbk. : alk. paper) -- ISBN 978-1-938063-11-4 (electronic) (print) -- ISBN 1-938063-11-2 (electronic) (print)
 [1. Schools--Fiction. 2. Friendship--Fiction. 3. Bullies--Fiction. 4. Oregon--Fiction.] I. DeYoe, Aaron, illustrator. II. DeYoe, Katie, illustrator. III. Title.
 PZ7.P2432Mi 2013
 [Fic]--dc23
                2012031518

Printed in Canada
Distributed by Publishers Group West

First edition

10 9 8 7 6 5 4 3 2 1

This is for Eli and Mark.
And for Sadie, *le lecteur d'infinité.*

CAST of CHARACTERS

QUINN ANDREWS-LEE

MICKEY ANDREWS-LEE
QUINN'S SISTER

JIM ANDREWS
QUINN'S DAD

MARION LEE
QUINN'S MOM

NEALLY RAY
STANDWELL

BRYAN STANDERS
NEALLY'S DAD

TABLE of CONTENTS

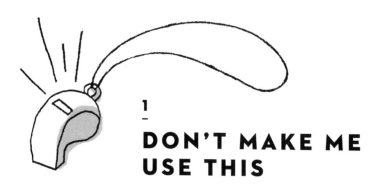

1
DON'T MAKE ME USE THIS

I bet it's against the rules to turn invisible, even for one second. Or explode into a bajillion pieces and reassemble across the playground—that would get you the whistle, for sure.

"HEY, QUINN, OVER HERE!"

Quinn Andrews-Lee bounced a four square ball against the blacktop and pretended he hadn't heard his name being called.

"QUINN! HEY, QUINNY QUINN-QUINN!"

Quinn ambled toward the drinking fountain. He was determined to ignore the persistent, louder-than-loud hollering behind him, even though he realized that ignorance was futile when it came to the hyper-human commotion that was Kelsey King.

"QUINN, THE BALL! YO, DORK-LEE, PASS IT OR STASH IT!"

Quinn took a sip of water. Gazing up at the stone gray clouds, he wondered which would be the bigger

......

1

waste of time: wishing for a snowstorm, or for the day when Kelsey would say something—anything—without bellowing like a rampaging elephant.

Kelsey caught up to Quinn and parked herself behind him, her thick fists planted firmly on her hips. "YOU'RE HOGGING PLAYGROUND EQUIPMENT ALL TO YOURSELF! THAT'S AGAINST THE RULES AND EVERYBODY KNOWS IT! MIZ BARNES! MIZ BARNES!" Kelsey's long, stringy, pasty-blond hair lashed against her cheeks as she hopped about and waved her hands in a manic effort to attract the attention of the playground supervisor. "QUINN'S JUST STANDING THERE KEEPING A PERFECTLY GOOD FOUR SQUARE BALL ALL TO HIMSELF!"

"Yee-ouch!" Quinn clapped his hands over his ears. Kelsey snatched the ball before it hit the ground and ran toward the gym.

"YOU CAN PLAY WALL-BALL WITH US," Kelsey hollered over her shoulder, "BUT NOT ON *MY* TEAM."

"Like I'd even want to be on your team," Quinn grumbled. He checked his watch; recess was over in ten minutes. He surveyed the playground, hoping to catch sight of fellow fifth graders amidst the packs of scurrying second and third graders that swarmed like bees around the tetherball and four square courts, and spotted Tay and Sam by the parallel bars. "Hey, guys!" Quinn jogged toward his friends.

"Running on the field *only*!" Ms. Barnes raised her whistle. "Don't make me use this!"

Quinn slowed to a fast walk and guiltily waved at the playground supervisor.

"Don't make her use that." Sam pinched his fingers together and blew an imaginary whistle. "Taylor Denton the Third got benched for the entire lunch recess the last time he made Ms. Barnes use her wicked devil whistle."

"No way!" Tay elbowed Sam.

"Way!" Sam pushed Tay back against one of the parallel bars.

"I can get you in trouble, Samuel Jefferson Washington," Tay said. "I can get you in giga-billion trouble; in your-Daddy-gotta-call-the-lawyer trouble."

"How's that?" Quinn asked.

"I could get him expelled for actually playing on the playground." Tay pretended to bonk his head against one of the parallel bars.

Quinn tapped one of the cold metal bars. "Does anyone ever use these things?"

"Sure," Sam said. "My sister's sixth-grade class used to do gymnastics on the bars."

"Let's play wall-ball," Quinn suggested.

"No one's playing wall-ball," Tay said. "Not outside."

"There's a bunch of teams playing inside, in the gym," Quinn said. "We could be a team, the three of us, or we could join another team."

"Kelsey's in the gym; I can't be on her team because she doesn't like how I throw the ball." Sam pinched his nostrils together and spoke like a teacher giving a disparaging book report evaluation. "Mr. Washington, your windup and delivery is totally lacking in substance."

"That's not it—you can't be on her team 'cause you don't cheat," Tay snickered. "Besides, there's no way I'm playing in the gym. Ever heard Kelsey's outside voice when she's inside?"

"Ayiiiiiiiii!" Sam slapped his palms against his ears.

"Okay then, what do *you* want to do?" Quinn asked.

Tay scowled and shrugged his shoulders. Sam jammed his hands into his jacket pockets, shuffled his feet from side to side, and grinned halfheartedly at Quinn.

Quinn inspected the sky. The billowing clouds were neither puffy nor gray enough to imply an imminent storm of any significance, and this realization made him sigh. "It seems like we should get snow in December."

"Why should it seem that?" Tay asked. "We never get any snow."

"We did three years ago, in second grade, remember?" Sam said. "My sisters used to get snow days. Dad says we get snow about once every three years."

"Yeah, we get maybe an inch of snow," Tay snorted. "Big deal."

"It is for here," Quinn said. "Two more days of school and we're out. It would be so great to have a snowstorm during winter break."

"My dad grew up ..."

"In Minnesota," Tay finished Sam's sentence. "The entire planet knows this."

"Dad loves weather, probably because ..." Sam grinned at Tay, "they got a lot of it in that state where the entire planet knows he grew up. He watches all the weather channels; he says they're predicting a chance of snow if the temperature drops." Sam kicked the toe of Quinn's sneakers. "What'll we do while we wait for the snowstorm of the century?"

"Well," Quinn began, "we could ..."

"Yo, Tay!"

Matt Barker rocketed a muddy four square ball at Tay's stomach. Tay deflected it with his hands; the ball hit one of the parallel bars and rebounded toward Quinn, who caught it on the second bounce. Matt ran

......

behind Quinn and punched the ball, which flew out of Quinn's hands and rolled toward the bark chips surrounding the play structure. Matt ran after the ball, snarling, "Back off!" to a second-grade girl who leaned down to grab the ball.

"How come Ms. Barnes never catches *him* running?" Quinn muttered.

Matt held the ball against his hip, ran his fingers through his spiky blond hair and sauntered back to where Tay and Sam and Quinn stood. "C'mon, Tay. You, me, and Josh can whip Kelsey and her wall-ball whimps. Where's that Whistle Witch?" He looked around for the playground supervisor; Ms. Barnes was standing in front of the swing set, scolding two third graders. Matt whacked Tay's arm and the two boys ran toward the gym.

Sam swept his arm forward, bowed toward the gym and emulated a crisp, upper-crust British accent. "Ever so nice to see you, Master Barker."

"It's 'wimps,' not *whimps*," Quinn said. "What a jerk."

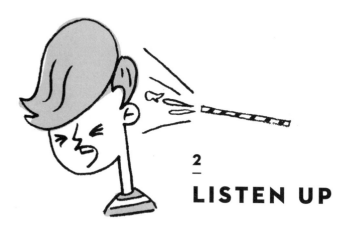

2
LISTEN UP

Click click, click click.

Ms. Blakeman raised her olive green, metallic frog clicker above her head. "Fifth graders, listen up!" *Click click, click click.* "Six minutes left until lunch. All those doing social studies units, wrap up your report outlines. All of you silent readers, get your bookmarks and find a stopping point."

Quinn felt a paper wad hit the back of his shirt, and heard Matt and Josh snickering from the row behind him. He placed a bookmark in chapter two of *Sorcerers and Gallantry: Medieval English Mythology* and tried not to sigh out loud at the massive injustice that was the student body makeup of his classroom.

It was, simply and profoundly, unfair. Every September, at the first assembly, Principal Shirkner fingered his signature red and blue polka dot bow tie while he gave the same boring speech about achievement, and how everyone was working to make Turner Creek the finest elementary school in Oregon. And every June, at the last assembly, with the teachers sitting up front and grinning at his every word, Shirkner fingered yet another one of his bow ties while he gave yet another boring speech about how the teachers had enjoyed their classes and would pick the best groupings of students for next year's classes. And every year since kindergarten Quinn had ended up in the worst class in Turner Creek Elementary: the class with Matt Barker in it.

Quinn was so intent on pondering his bad luck that he missed the distinctive squeak of the classroom door. He lifted his desktop, stashed his book, and retrieved his lunch bag, only then realizing that the whispering had risen to a level that usually summoned Ms. Blakeman's frog clicker.

Teena Freeman's desk was directly in front of Quinn's. She turned around and whispered, "I'm glad it's not me."

"What's not you?" Quinn asked.

Teena pointed to the front of the class. Ms. Blakeman was speaking softly to the three people who had entered her classroom: a man, a woman, and a girl. The man had his arm draped around the girl's shoulders, and the woman lightly touched the girl's hair. Ms. Blakeman shook hands with the girl.

"It's hard enough being a new kid in September." Teena wiped her nose against the sleeve of her dingy, once-white shirt. "But two days before winter break, and right before lunch?"

"We're getting a new student?" Quinn asked.

"Duh. Oh, no!" Teena groaned. "They kissed her goodbye, in front of everyone!"

"I do so look forward to getting to know you." Ms. Blakeman beamed her Open House smile at the two adults as they exited her classroom.

Click click, click click.

"Fifth graders, listen up! Please give your best Turner Creek welcome to our new class member." Ms. Blakeman looked down at the folder she held and her eyeglasses slid down her nose. She adjusted her glasses and opened the folder. "Nelly Standwell comes to us from Spokane, Washington. Oh, fantastic! It says that Mr. Standers, Nelly's father, will volunteer ..."

"It's *Neally*, not Nelly," the new girl interrupted.

"Excuse me; Neally?" Ms. Blakeman took a pen from her pocket and wrote in the folder.

"That's all right." The girl looked around the room, right to left and front to back, as if she were memorizing every face in the class. "Most people get it wrong at first. Neally; it rhymes with really. My name is Neally Ray Standwell, and it's nice to meet all of you."

Matt covered his mouth with his hands. "It's nice to meet y'all," he said, in a muffled, high-pitched whine. Josh let loose with the snorting noises he made when he was supposedly laughing, but which Quinn had always thought sounded like pigs choking on their slop.

Click click, click click.

"Fifth graders!" Ms. Blakeman glared in the direction of the laughter. Matt pulled himself up in his chair and sat as straight as a number two pencil. He jerked his chin in Josh's direction, his blue eyes twinkling at Ms. Blakeman as if to say, "Can you believe that clown?"

"I'm sorry to rush the introduction," Ms. Blakeman said. "We'll do more after lunch, but we need to get going. Fifth graders, you know the drill; let's help Neally figure it out. Hot-lunchers and milk-onlys in front, cold-lunchers in the back. Arturo, you are line leader today."

Neally Ray Standwell. That has to be the coolest name ever, Quinn thought. He got in step with the other milk-onlys, so lost in thought that he neglected to see that that the Coolest Name Ever was right behind him.

"Hotters? Colders? Milk-only-ers? Are these some kind of tag team names?"

The new girl's voice gave no clue as to whether she was teasing. Quinn turned to answer her, and felt his cheeks begin to flush. He spun back around and faced the door.

"Hello there," Neally said to Quinn's back.

"Hi," Quinn said to his shoes. The line began to move toward the cafeteria.

"So, what is the deal and which one are you? I mean, about this lunch-line march."

"Hot-lunchers get lunch at the cafeteria," Quinn replied without turning to look at her. "Cold-lunchers bring their lunch from home. Milk-onlys bring their lunch but get milk at the cafeteria. We all go to the cafeteria, then come back and eat at our desks, then it's lunch recess."

"You have to eat lunch in the classroom?"

"We get fifteen minutes to eat at our desks," Quinn explained. "Sometimes only ten, if we don't ... ah, foof!" The line stopped at the cafeteria door. "We're supposed to be ahead of Mrs. Franklin's class. If you're not here exactly at your time they let the next class in ahead of you."

"My fault, I suppose, that your class is late. The introduction and all. So sorry."

Quinn didn't think Neally sounded so sorry, or any sorry at all.

"Anyway, you have to eat lunch at your desk?"

Quinn nodded. "I guess because it rains so much."

"Well, it rains in Spokane too," Neally said. "It

snows, even. But most days we still got to eat outside, on the picnic tables under the shelters."

"We have shelters," Quinn said. "Half of the blacktop is under shelters. But no picnic tables. Those are ..."

"No picnic tables under the shelters? That's what shelters are *for*. Anyway, what's so big about a little rain?"

"Yeah! It's not like ..." Quinn took a deep breath and decided not to finish agreeing with the new girl. He'd always thought the eat-at-your-desk rule was unreasonable, but hearing it criticized from this stranger who had been at Turner Creek Elementary for a whole ten minutes suddenly made him feel like putting his arm around his school.

"Eating inside's not so bad. You can push your desk together with three others in your row." Quinn turned to face Neally. "Sometimes you get a buddy lunch. That's when you can pick anyone in class, no matter where you both sit, and you get to eat by the teacher's ..."

Quinn's throat felt ripply, like the time when he had laryngitis and missed two days of school. He wasn't used to anyone looking at him so intently. Usually when someone stared at him it was because he had food stuck in his teeth or because they were mad at him. Neally stared at Quinn as if he were about to say something incredible, but Quinn couldn't tell if she expected him to say something incredibly interesting or incredibly stupid. Her eyes were deep and serious, and the strangest color of brown—no, they were green! They were a green so dark, it couldn't be a natural, eye-color green. It was a green from another era, or another galaxy; it was *cosmos green*.

"Buddy lunch, uh, you eat by the teacher's desk," Quinn heard himself saying. "It's a privilege. You can earn it by …"

"Move along, milkies." Matt stumbled out the cafeteria door, pretending he was about to spill his tray.

"Ay, hey!" Arturo Delgado turned around, dipped his head three times and cupped his hand, motioning to Quinn. "Going now."

Quinn saw that he had lagged several feet behind Arturo, who hesitated in front of the entrance to the cafeteria, waiting for the rest of the class to catch up. Quinn also saw that a straw had rolled off of Matt's tray. He bent over and picked up the straw from the footprint-streaked, speckled tile floor, mumbling to himself about how once again Matt had somehow managed to sneak to the front of the line without getting caught.

"My straw—oh, stop, you *thief*!" Matt's yell was shrill, like a cartoon damsel in distress. He lunged toward Quinn, but Neally quickly stepped between the two boys, whisked the straw from Quinn's grasp, and twirled it above her head as if the straw was a Fourth of July sparkler.

Matt shoved his lunch tray toward Neally. "You're welcome," Neally said. She held the straw loosely, dangling it between her thumb and forefinger as if to drop it on his tray. Matt jerked the tray back, and the straw remained in her hand. Neally arched her feet, standing tip-toed, which made her a good six inches taller than Matt. She looked down at Matt, her galaxy-green eyes boring into his.

She's expecting something, Quinn thought. It looked like there would be a stare-down. How was a new girl to know that in all of infinity, Matt Barker had never lost a stare-down?

"*Ándele!*" Arturo nervously whispered to Quinn. "C'mon!"

"You dropped something," Neally said to Matt.

"No kidding," Matt sneered.

Neally slowly and methodically blinked her eyes and tapped the straw against her palm.

"MOVE IT UP!" Kelsey boomed from the end of the line.

"Thank you, ma'am," Matt finally said to Neally.

Neally dropped the straw on Matt's tray. "You're welcome." Her voice was warm, but there was no smile in her eyes, and her fiery green irises seemed to turn a bitter, deep blue as she watched Matt saunter away. Quinn watched Neally as she stared at Matt's retreating form, and he felt as if Ms. Blakeman's frog clicker had snapped between his ears. There was something familiar and unsettling about Neally's expression, something that reminded him of a shimmering green python, the kind of snake that was on the cover of his sister's favorite picture book. Neally had eyes that saw inside you, even when they seemed to look right past you.

That's it! She knows.

Quinn's face felt hot, and he knew that anyone who looked at him would see him blushing.

3

THE WORMS GO IN, THE WORMS GO OUT

The mud-matted, thick green blades jutted defiantly skyward, as if taunting the school district's groundskeeper, *I dare you to cut me down.* Turner Creek Elementary School's field was in need of a good mowing, Quinn thought, as he stood at the edge of the playground blacktop. He considered running a lap or two around the field, but didn't want to attract attention by sprinting solo. When they were heading to recess, Tay, Sam, and Quinn had all agreed to organize a game of tag, but as soon as they got outside, Tay said he wanted to go rescue the swing set from the second graders, and Sam had followed Tay.

Quinn couldn't decide which he liked least—the swings, or Tay's recently acquired interest in the swings. Quinn had known Taylor Denton III since kindergarten. It used to be that Tay was always up for playing tag, but now he just wanted to play that stupid game where you try to swing higher than anyone else, high enough that the swing chain loses tension at the top of your arc and jerks you back on the downswing, high enough to attract the attention of Ms. Barnes, who blows her whistle and yells, "It's dangerous to swing that high. You're setting a bad example for the younger kids, and if you fall and break your neck, your parents will sue the school!" at which point you slow down and sing that stupid song:

> *The worms go in, the worms go out*
> *in your stomach and out your snout*
> *they eat your guts with sauerkraut.*

Quinn had been bored with that game since third grade, and he thought that Tay's newfound interest had more to do with annoying the younger kids than with using the swings. Tay wants to get to the swings before the second graders do, Quinn told Sam, because he likes to watch them make their pathetic lost puppy faces and beg for a turn. Sam agreed with Quinn, but lately it seemed to Quinn that whenever Tay wanted to go on the swings—whenever Tay wanted to do anything—Sam went along with Tay.

Arturo Delgado, Janos Petrov, and Lily L'Sotho stood at the far end of the blacktop with their hands in their coat pockets, bouncing up and down on their toes. The

three friends and ESL study-group mates moved as
if they were one entity, and gazed longingly out at the
field, wondering how muddy their shoes might get if
they chanced running on the grass. Quinn scanned the
school yard. Everyone else was either playing tetherball
or four square or some other group game. He reminded
himself that first-rate English speaking skills were not
necessary for tag. Perhaps if he got something started,
others would join in. Quinn jogged onto the field and
sure enough, Arturo ran to join him, followed by Lily
and Janos.

"FREEZE TAG!" Kelsey King jumped off the top
of the play structure slide and ran toward the field,
followed by four younger students. "DON'T START
WITHOUT ME!"

"We'll be a team." Quinn pointed to Arturo, Lily, and
Janos. "The four of us, okay?"

"YOU'RE IT!" Kelsey flew past Quinn and whacked
her hand against his shoulder. The students who
followed Kelsey shrieked with joy, and scattered across
the field like a pack of squirrels let loose on a peanut
farm.

Lily clapped her hands and ran aimlessly in a figure
eight, looking for someone to tag.

"No, *I'm* it!" Quinn called to Lily. "You're supposed to
round up the others for *me* to tag!"

Janos stood as if frozen to the spot, his thick, straw-yellow, bowl-over-the-head-cut bangs almost obscuring his eyes. He stretched his arms out like a scarecrow and turned slowly in a circle, his gap-toothed grin splitting his face from ear to ear.

"This is great," Quinn muttered, as one of Kelsey's squirrels hopped in front of Quinn, wiggled her hands by her ears and made a *nyah-nyah* face. "C'mon, Arturo," Quinn yelled to his teammate, "chase 'em toward me."

SSSSSSSSSSSSSQQQQQQ QQQQQQQQQQQQQQUUUU UUUUUUUURRRRRRK!

Ms. Barnes' whistle sliced through the chilly noon air.

"No running on ..."

"IT'S THE *FIELD*!" Kelsey sprinted to the edge of the grass. She shook her fists and stomped her feet, spattering mud on her jeans. "WE CAN RUN ON THE FIELD!"

"Not after three days of rain!" Ms. Barnes yelled back. "All of you, here, now." The tag players reluctantly shuffled toward the blacktop. "You're ruining the track marks." Ms. Barnes pointed her whistle toward the line of flattened mud and grass that formed an oval inside the borders of the field. "The sixth graders have to do timed laps next week for their P.E. grade."

"But next week is winter break," Quinn protested.

"The next week of *school*." Ms. Barnes spoke slowly, as if she were trying to explain cursive writing to an orangutan. "The school can't afford to pay the groundskeeper to come back during vacation and redo the lines."

Ms. Barnes craned her neck toward the sounds of a *Did too! Did not!* argument, her eyes gleaming with anticipation as she stuck the tip of her whistle in her mouth. She marched toward the tetherball courts, her brawny arms swinging and her purple plastic clogs squeaking with every step. Kelsey stuck her tongue out at Ms. Barnes' back, and she and her squirrels scampered toward the play structure, walking as fast as they could without breaking into a run.

"*Gracias*, Quinn." Arturo tugged at the spiky, coal-black, close-cropped hair behind his ear and smiled shyly. "I like tag." Arturo headed for the gym, with Lily and Janos right behind him, as usual.

I bet they even go to the bathroom together, Quinn thought. *Well, maybe not Lily.*

I hope it rains the first week of winter break, and then during the second week I'll come here with twenty other kids and we'll run on the field every day.

4
MICKEY GETS ANTY

Quinn pushed teriyaki chicken and sesame noodles around his plate with his fork while his sister Mickey entertained their parents with the day's events in Ms. Reese's second-grade class.

"*Three* kids had their names written on the chalkboard. That's the most ever!" Mickey exclaimed. She dropped her fork on her plate, pushed her chin-length hair behind her ears and wriggled her stubby fingers in front of her mouth. "Ms. Reese says when there's only two days left 'til vacation everyone gets anty."

"Antsy," Quinn groused. "No one gets anty, they get antsy."

"You sound thoughtful." Jim Andrews grinned across the table at his son. "Did anything interesting happen at school today?"

"Let me guess." Marion Lee turned to face Quinn, who sat next to her, and her foot playfully nudged

Quinn's shin under the table. "Matt Barker saw the error of his ways and came crawling to you on hands and knees, begging for your understanding and forgiveness."

"Mo-om!" Although he was in no joking mood, Quinn could not stop the smile that snuck across his face. "Like I'll live long enough to see that."

"Now let *me* guess," Mr. Andrews said. "Is there more trouble with Matt?"

"You still think he's trying to get Tay to be his friend, and not yours?" Ms. Lee asked.

"No. Well, sort of. Matt was being ... Matt." Quinn looked at his father, and then at his mother, and then down at his dinner plate in an attempt to quash a chuckle that caught him by surprise. His parents both had warm, coffee-brown, wide-set eyes and short, dark brown hair, and at that moment, with their softly arched eyebrows and almost identical facial expressions of loving concern, he thought they looked more like fraternal twins than a married couple.

Quinn usually enjoyed talking with his parents when he had a problem. Sometimes they had answers to questions he hadn't even asked yet, and sometimes they just listened and empathized. Either way, their attention always made him feel better. But Quinn had too many feelings stomping around in his brain; he didn't know how to make them line up single file, and he thought that if he let them all out they'd crash together and trip over his tongue, and he'd sound ridiculous, or worse.

Quinn was not looking forward to winter break. He didn't want to say that out loud and worry his parents; *every* adult thinks *every* kid looks forward to *every* vacation. Quinn was determined to look "on the brighted side," as Mickey put it. It was Mickey who had pointed out that two weeks of winter break would be a two-week break from Matt Barker. It was also Mickey who'd pointed out that while their family was staying put, all of Mickey's and Quinn's friends would be traveling during vacation. There would be no one to play with, except for Grandma and Grandpa Lee, who always came to stay with Quinn's family during the week between Christmas and New Year's. Grandma Lee was both soft-spoken and high-spirited, and although she claimed to be "allergic to the rain" she was willing to play checkers or cards or any indoor game with you all day long. Slow-moving, fast-talking Grandpa Lee knew more elephant and fart jokes than any kid at Quinn's school, and drew cool pictures of Chinese letters, but the noises he made when he chewed his toast drove Quinn up the wall. Quinn loved his mother's parents and looked forward to their visits; still, a week was a long time.

Quinn looked up from his plate. His parents still wore identical expressions, the one their eyebrows got taller and their eyes puffed up like baby spotted owls. It was the *You know you can tell me anything* face. It was a good face, Quinn reminded himself.

"We got a new student in class today, and she …"

"We got *two* new kids last week!" Mickey gestured wildly with her fork, not realizing that she'd flung noodles on the wall behind her. "And we're getting another …"

"Mickey," Ms. Lee said, "this isn't a contest. Let Quinn finish his story."

Mr. Andrews pushed his chair back, went into the kitchen and returned 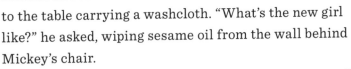 to the table carrying a washcloth. "What's the new girl like?" he asked, wiping sesame oil from the wall behind Mickey's chair.

"I'm not sure," Quinn said. "She didn't get there until just before lunch. She's … well … yeah. Her desk is up front. Ms. Blakeman's going to rearrange the desks after vacation."

"Something tells me the new girl made an impression," Ms. Lee said. "What's her name? Is she from around here?"

"She's from Spokane. She's tall, and talks like, I don't know, like she's smart." Quinn put down his fork. "I only talked with her a couple of times. She seems friendly, and she has these weird eyes. I've never seen eyes that color."

"Pink?!" Mickey squealed. "Are they pink, like Alice's? I'll get her and you can check."

"No animals at the table, no exceptions," Mr. Andrews said.

"Alice has red eyes." Quinn rolled his own eyes in disgust. "*White* rats have *red* eyes, not pink eyes. Okay, but now that you mention pets, I thought at first the new girl had dark brown eyes, like Peppy's."

"If I brought Peppy out of his cage, we could check?" Mickey looked hopefully at her father. "Since Alice is my pet and Peppy is Quinn's, maybe ..."

"You little negotiator." Marion Lee reached across the table and ruffled her daughter's hair.

"Nice try, Mickey," Mr. Andrews said. "No Peppy at the dinner table and no Alice. No hamsters, no rats, no animals."

"No fun," Mickey muttered.

"Her eyes are so dark, and *green*," Quinn said. "They're a color like you'd see in old paintings at the museum, or from another galaxy or cosmos, maybe. Neally has the greenest ..."

"Neally?"

Quinn nodded at his mother. "Really, it's Neally.

Neally Ray Standwell. Sam agrees with me: Neally has the coolest name ever. She even thinks so; it's obvious she likes her own name."

"So, the new kid has cosmic green eyes and the third best name ever," Ms. Lee said.

"Third best?" Mickey asked.

"It's a tie for first and second." Marion Lee grinned.

"I know, I know." Although Quinn had never seen any animal's lips form a genuine, human-like smile, he could tell his own mouth was twisting itself into the kind of grin adults said belonged on a sheep. He began to recite in a sing-song voice, "Mom thinks the best names in the world are Quinn Michael Andrews-Lee and Michelle ..."

"Mickey!" Mickey insisted.

"And Michelle *'Mickey'* Elizabeth Andrews-Lee."

Quinn looked past his parents, past the dining nook into the family room, to the framed pictures that cluttered the room's oak fireplace mantle. He loved the story his father told him every year, on Quinn's birthday, of how he was named for a special friend of his father's. The summer after James Andrews graduated from college, he made a bicycle trip across Ireland, where he met a man named Quinn Michael Tiernan. Although he looked nothing like his namesake, who had sapphire eyes and thick, wild hair the color of candied yams, Quinn liked looking at the picture of his father and the Irish Quinn. On a gravel road atop a moss-green hill, framed against an impossibly blue sky, the two friends straddled their bicycles, held their helmets above their heads, and laughed into the camera lens. "Aye and always," the Irish Quinn had written across the bottom of the photo. That meant *Friends for life*, Quinn's father said.

5
—
BECAUSE
SHE CAN

It had been the longest day of infinity. Quinn reminded himself that whatever happened on Friday would be the last whatever to happen before vacation. At nine a.m. Quinn took his last spelling test before vacation. The last morning recess before vacation was followed by *the-last-time-Brandon-Morley-needs-a-hall-pass-even-though-he-should-have-gone-to-the-bathroom-at-recess* before vacation. Before long, Quinn was standing in the last lunch line before vacation.

At lunch recess, Quinn decided to play a last game of four square before vacation. Quinn was not the only student who had this idea, and all four courts had long lines of kids waiting to rotate in. Quinn got into the shortest line, behind at least ten other kids, including Tay, Sam, and Josh, and the new girl, who was in front of Josh. All of the kids in line seemed to be focused on Neally and not the four square game; a few circled around her, seemingly unconcerned about keeping their place in line.

"You've got *great* eyes!" The voice was distressingly familiar to Quinn, but Tay blocked Quinn's view. Quinn leaned to the side to get a better view, and groaned. His sister was near the front of the line, standing—or rather, squirming with a star-struck admiration—between Neally and Matt.

"Ah, foof!" Quinn muttered. He didn't go out of his way to avoid his sister at school, but whenever he did let her join in a game with him and his friends, Matt would tell anyone with ears about how Quinn *liked* to play with whiny, brainless second graders. And here they were, Quinn and his sister, totally, completely, accidentally occupying the same four square line. Quinn briefly considered moving to another court.

No, this will be okay. It'll be the last line-I-wish-I-wasn't-standing-in before vacation.

"Your eyes are so green!" Mickey gushed. "I bet there's no other green like it in this world. It's another galaxy green!"

Quinn cringed to hear his copycat sister. No one else could know that Mickey was repeating his unique observation; still, it felt like she'd stolen his opinion.

"Thank you," Neally said. "Both of my parents have green eyes, which is unusual."

"Whooo-wee, *green* eyes, how unusual," Matt said.

"Like two green grapes smashed in your face. Hey, that's not a bad idea." Matt fumbled through his jacket pocket, as if he had something stashed there. "Where's my lunch leftovers?"

Josh slapped Matt on the back and laughed, which was no surprise, but Tay began to laugh too. Quinn bit his lip to keep himself from chastising his friend. How could Tay join in on teasing the new girl?

Matt gave a thumbs-up to Tay and raised his hand in the air. "Ducks rule, Beavers drool!" The boys exchanged a high-five.

"Ducks rule, beavers drool?" Neally repeated.

"It's a dumb sports thing," Mickey whispered to Neally.

"I suppose," Neally said thoughtfully, "any sport that involves drooling animals could be considered dumb."

"No, it's not the animals that drool ..."

"It's the people who watch them?"

Mickey began to laugh, then clapped her hand over her mouth and leaned closer to Neally. "It's the teams' names. Ducks are the team from one college and Beavers are the team from another. If kids' parents went to one school they say that their team rules, and they make fun of the other team ..."

"Which drools?" Neally guessed.

Mickey nodded. "Our parents didn't go to those colleges, so we don't care about silly stuff like that."

She glanced over her shoulder and lowered her voice.
"Quinn's teacher went to the college that has the Beaver
team, so he says he's a Beaver fan. But he's really not.
He just says that 'cause he likes his teacher. Matt's and
Josh's and Tay's dads went to the other school, and ..."

"Why are you whispering?" Neally asked.

"'Cause kids who like those teams get mad if they
think you're making fun of them."

"Oh, powers that be, I am so frightened! I
certainly don't want a mad duck in pursuit of me."
Neally wriggled her fingers in front of her mouth and
knocked her knees together. "Say, have you ever played
doubles in four square? It's way fun. Want to try it when
we get in?"

"Really?" Mickey gasped. "You'd be on a team with
me?"

"Sure. We can get everyone to double up. If you don't
have a partner in mind you can just choose the person
standing next to you."

"She's in the second grade, you know," Josh said to
Neally.

"Second grade?" Neally scrunched up her nose and
thoughtfully stroked her chin. "Let me see, that's the
grade between first and third, correct?"

Josh looked confused, as if he'd asked Neally her age
and she'd replied, "Canada."

Neally turned back to Mickey. "We haven't been
formally introduced," she said. "My name is ..."

......

"Neally Ray Standwell!" Mickey said. "I heard about you."

Several kids standing in line turned to look at Quinn, who decided it would be a good time to retie his shoelaces.

"Neally Ray Standwell, you have the coolest name ever!" Mickey declared. "And that's ever in the history of all of the names of namehood."

"Yeah, right," Matt snorted. He'd moved up to first in line, but ignored the open spot on the court. "Neally Standwell—what kind of name is that?" He hunched his shoulders up around his ears, leaned forward so that his knuckles grazed the ground, furrowed his brow, and jutted his chin out, in a passable imitation of the caveman pictured on Ms. Blakeman's classroom anthropology chart. "Me Neally," Matt grunted. "Me stand well. But me sit bad."

Matt's cave man grumble devolved into a fit of high-pitched laughter, to which Josh and Tay eagerly contributed. Sam looked embarrassed, and Quinn merely looked away, while Mickey looked as if someone had thrown mud on her birthday cake.

"Sit bad! Stand well, sit bad!" Josh doubled over and slapped his hands on his thighs. Although the look on Josh's face suggested laughter, the noises he produced were peculiar, clacking whinnies, as if he'd inhaled a Shetland pony.

"Anyone know the Heimlich maneuver?" Neally patted Josh's shoulder. "Don't worry, Josh, we'll go to the office and call 9-1-1. I'm certain the paramedics can get that wiener dog—or whatever is stuck in your throat—out of there in no time."

Three kids on the four square court were waiting for a fourth. "Next in line, c'mon!" the server called out. "Hey, Matt, rotate in."

"Your name is Matt?" Neally asked.

"Indeed," Sam said, flourishing his hand. "You have the honor of speaking with the Right Master Matthew Mark Luke John Barker, son of the Right Reverend ..."

"Yeah," Matt shot Sam a withering glance, "it's Matt."

"Hey Mickey, I have a joke for you," Neally said.

"Is it a knock-knock joke?" Mickey asked.

"Even better. What do you call a boy with no arms and legs who's sprawled on your front porch? Matt!"

Quinn couldn't decipher the expression on Matt's face. He was well-acquainted with Mad Matt, Cruel

Matt, and Smiley-Face-When-The-Adults-Are-Looking Matt, but he didn't recognize Embarrassed Matt.

Matt glared at Neally with a smoldering, silent gaze for a few seconds. Then he turned his back on her and joined the four square game.

"You're in trouble," Mickey warned Neally. "He's mean."

"So what?" Neally looked down the line, making eye contact with and dipping her chin in acknowledgement to each student who stood in line behind her. "So what, right?"

"So, this is what." Quinn tapped his watch. "I don't think we'll get to play."

Mickey grinned at Neally. "So what?"

"Sew buttons on your underwear, that's what!" Neally said.

Mickey giggled and tried to tickle Neally, who grabbed Mickey's hands and giggled, "Aha, gotcha!"

"Hey, who made your shirt?" Mickey pulled her hands out of Neally's grasp. "The tag is sewed backwards."

Quinn looked at Neally's shirt and saw the outline of a clothing tag under the front collar.

"The tag is where it's supposed to be. I'm wearing my shirt backwards."

"Oh, I've done that before, lots of times," Mickey said. "You can fix it in the bathroom. I'll save your place in line."

"No, thanks, it's intentional. Sometimes I wear my shirts this way."

"Why would you wear your shirts that way?" Tay asked.

"Because I can." Neally smiled a curious smile, chirped, "See ya around, cutie" to Mickey, and skipped toward the drinking fountain.

"I SHOULDA KNOWN THIS WOULD BE THE SLOWEST LINE!"

"Who's gonna double with Kelsey?" Tay groaned, not bothering to turn around to see who had joined the line.

"Matt and Josh are playing easies, so no one else can get in," Quinn informed Kelsey. "This could go on forever, and we've only got a few minutes of recess left. Let's play wall-ball."

"It's too cold for wall-ball." Tay pulled his jacket tighter. "Let's go to the swings."

"Uh, Tay," Quinn said, "it'll be even colder swinging on the ..."

"Four square is boring to infinity." Matt snuck up behind Tay and bounced the four square ball off his head. "Wall-ball in the gym! Last one inside plays on a team by himself!"

The four square line disintegrated before Quinn's eyes as all of the kids, Tay and Sam included, followed Matt to the gym. Only Mickey remained behind. She picked up the ball and looked at her brother, her eyes widening with hope and sympathy.

"It's all right, Quinn."

Quinn didn't know what felt worse: being deserted by your so-called friends, or having your little sister try to make you feel better because she'd seen your so-called friends desert you.

"Let's ask Mom if she'll take us to the pool," Mickey suggested. "There's nothing like a swim after a hard day at school, except for … well, except for a swim after a hard day at school. Okey dokey?"

The buzzer rang out, signaling the end of lunch recess.

"That's getting to be *soooo* loud!"

"Mickey, you say that every time the lunch buzzer rings. It's the same buzzer as always."

Mickey tilted her head, touching her ear to her shoulder. She did that, Quinn thought, whenever a new idea was trying to enter her head and the old ones didn't want to make room.

"Really? It still sounds louder." Mickey headed for the wall where the second graders lined up. She turned around and called back to her brother. "Say, do you ever wonder if someone counted to six thousand hundred thousand, and they were still alive?"

Quinn knew she didn't expect an answer. Whenever Mickey wore that quizzical face at home, Quinn and his mom would play a game. His mom would say, "Mickey's thinking out loud," and Quinn would circle his finger by his ear and say, "*Think*–ing; *that's* what you call it."

For just one microscopic moment Quinn wished he was back in the second grade. Although he rarely missed an opportunity to tease her, Quinn sometimes felt envious of Mickey, in ways he didn't understand. His father said that Quinn admired Mickey's positive attitude, but it was more than that, Quinn thought. Or, it was different than that.

YOOOOWEEE!

Matt Barker's distinctive yelp bounced off the walls and ricocheted off the roof of the playground cover down to the blacktop, and Quinn had his last figuring-something-out-moment before vacation: It's not that Mickey is "positive," or that nothing bothers her—it's that nothing bothers her for longer than two minutes. That characteristic seems to make her happy, Quinn grudgingly admitted to himself, but he knew that not letting something bother you means you aren't fully paying attention.

Quinn Andrews-Lee had figured something out long before any vacation: if you pay the least bit of attention in life, things will bother you for a lot longer than a couple of lousy minutes.

6
QUINN PAYS ATTENTION

Ms. Blakeman's class was the first class to be let out for vacation. Quinn was the first student out the door, and thus was the first student to discover that while the diligent scholars of Turner Creek Elementary were cleaning out their desks, the first snow in three years had fallen in Hillsboro, Oregon.

He let out his breath in a frosty gasp. Less than an inch of snow dusted the ground and the rhododendrons by the main building, but the stuff was glistening and white—it was snow! Quinn's classmates pushed past him, gleefully kicking at the light powder beneath their feet. Ms. Barnes, who was bus monitor as well as playground supervisor, stood ramrod straight at the spot by the curb where students lined up for their busses.

Quinn set his book pack down and began to scoop up snow in his hand, and a cold, wet blob hit the top of his jacket and slid down his neck. "Hey!" he gasped.

Teena Freeman crouched behind Quinn, trying very hard to look like she had not thrown the snowball. Quinn cupped his hands to press clumps of white mush into a respectable sphere. It wasn't much, but it would have to do. As soon as the meager missile left his hand he heard Ms. Barnes' whistle blast, which felt icier than the slush down his back.

"The next one who throws a snowball goes to Shirkner's office. You! *BRRRREEEEET!*" Ms. Barnes aimed her whistle at Neally, who was gathering a pile of snow. "Drop it, now!"

"Oh, for Santa's sake! Let the kids play in the snow."

Quinn looked to see who had dared to talk back to the whistle. The voice belonged to a man who stood at the curb, behind Ms. Barnes. It was the man who'd come to class with Neally.

Ms. Barnes looked like she'd swallowed her whistle. Her cheeks and nose were red, as if she'd been sunburned. Quinn wondered if it were true that, as some of the sixth graders had said, Ms. Barnes had the power to cancel recess for adults.

"There could be rocks in the snowballs!" Ms. Barnes huffed.

"Rocks?" Neally's father repeated.

"This is a safety issue. If kids scoop up snow from the ground they might also scoop up rocks or other sharp objects. What if there was broken glass

underneath, or rusty nails, or
razor blades? A kid would
get hit in the eye with it,
that's what."

The man ran his
fingers through his
beard, and his eyes
sparkled as if Ms.
Barnes had told him
the funniest joke in infinity.

Neally ran to her father. "I know, I know; no running
in the snow," she said as she passed Ms. Barnes.

"C'mon." Neally's father enveloped his daughter in
a bear hug and then took her hand in his. "Let's go out
and make some rocky razor snowballs."

Although Quinn's back was wet, he didn't feel cold.
He watched Neally walk hand in hand with her father,
and for the first time in a long time Quinn felt that
Something Else could happen, if you paid attention.
Maybe, just possibly, life could actually change. Even if
he'd have to wait a whole two weeks to find out.

7

FAMOUS
CARROT DIVER

Click click, click click.

Ms. Blakeman looked out over a sea of students fidgeting at their desks. She pushed her glasses up the bridge of her nose and raised her clicker over her head. "My first click of the new year. How exciting that must be for you all! Seriously," Ms. Blakeman continued, amidst her students' groans and giggles, "it's good to see you. I'd love to hear your stories from winter break. Oh yes, I've got it." Ms. Blakeman lowered her chin, and her glasses slithered down her nose. "We'll get those back-to-school jitters *out* by putting them *down*. Fifth graders, pencils and paper! While I'm passing out spelling lists and going over your monthly planners, please give me two paragraphs on ..." She raised her head, as if listening for a barely audible bird call. "Anyone care to guess?"

"What I did on my winter vacation," several students grumbled.

"Ah, the incomparable joy that comes from teaching the gifted!" Ms. Blakeman smiled so hard her eyes disappeared into the tops of her puffy pink cheeks.

Quinn wrote his name at the top of his paper, chewed the end of his pencil eraser, and looked around the classroom. The new seating arrangement wasn't a drastic change; Ms. Blakeman had kept the reading groups together. Matt Barker was still too close for comfort—in the row ahead of him, where Teena used to sit—but Sam was next to Quinn, on the left. Tay sat behind Sam, next to Neally. Yes, the girl with the coolest name ever was now seated directly in back of him, and Quinn suddenly wondered what he looked like from behind. What if his underwear tag was sticking out?

Quinn peeked at Sam's paper. Other than his name, the date, and the title, "The Glorious Holiday Escapades of Samuel Jefferson Washington," Sam had written nothing. It seemed to Quinn that most of the students were doing what he was doing: staring at the papers of the students nearby, trying to pass the time until morning recess.

"There's nothing there."

Quinn quickly covered his paper with his hands, but Neally was speaking to Sam, not him.

"Your page is blank," Neally persisted.

"Kinda like his brain," Tay said.

"Insult alert, insult alert." Sam sounded like a robot with a sinus infection. "Must hold on to self-esteem."

"Didn't you and your family go on a ski trip over the break?" Neally asked. "That should give you a lot to write about."

"My mom and dad and sisters like to ski, but I'm not into it," Sam said. "I can't think of what to write. Anyway, it's just busywork. It's more fun to draw it."

"You're gonna draw your vacation?" Tay yawned. "Another comic strip, how original."

Ms. Blakeman was at the front row, leaning over Arturo's desk. She raised her arm. *Click click, click click.* "Fifth graders! I'll allow some leeway on the first day back, but keep the chatter level down to a quiet roar."

"Samuel Jefferson Washington?" Neally tapped her pencil on Sam's paper.

"He signs all his papers that way," Teena murmured.

"It's his name," added Tay.

"But everyone calls you Sam," Neally said to Sam. "Even the teacher."

"Righty-o," said Sam.

"Then, why not just write, 'Sam Washington?'"

"My parents are history teachers," Sam said. "Both of them." He drew the outline of a comic strip on his paper.

"Your parents are history teachers." Neally's voice indicated she did not consider that to be a satisfactory explanation. "And your point would be?"

"It's a mystery." Sam drew a picture of a stick man on skis.

"They want his full name on all his papers," Tay said. "Every year on Back to School Night they have to explain it to the new teacher. I'm so glad my folks aren't teachers."

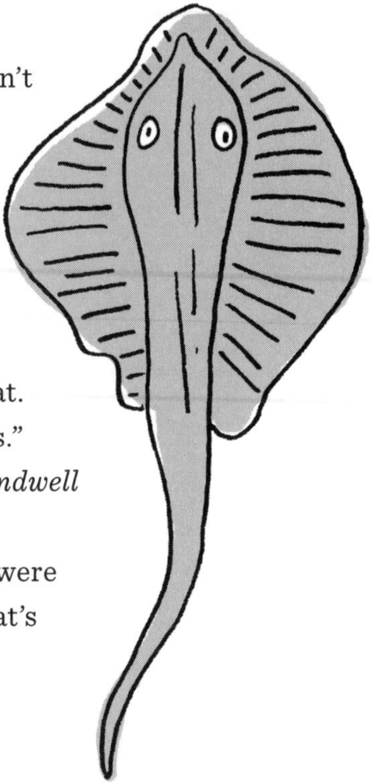

"I'd never sign my middle name," Teena declared. "I don't know why I even have to write my last name; I'm the only Teena in class. How do you sign your name, Neally?"

"First and last. But I am considering changing that. New year, new arrangements." Neally wrote *Neally Ray Standwell* at the top of her paper.

"I wish my middle name were shorter," Teena sighed. "What's 'Ray' for?"

"For me."

"No, I mean ..."

"I know what you mean." Neally smiled. "It's just my middle name. My mom says it was for a stingray she saw when she was snorkeling in the Caribbean. Dad says it's for a beam of light, like a ray of sunshine. I like the story about the stingray best. Have you ever seen one?"

"Only in a video," Teena said. "But I'm going to see a live one someday. I'm going to go to Hawaii and go snorkeling. Jeff said he'd teach me."

"Who's Jeff? Your older brother?"

"My mom's boyfriend." Teena's cheeks turned scarlet, and she got a thinking-hard look on her face. "The last one, I mean. Not the one she has now."

Quinn was bewildered by the Neally and Teena conversation. Pasty-faced, toothpick-thin, timid Teena was not normally a talker, with anyone. Two sentences was her limit, and then she'd start humming to herself and spinning her hair. Teena's thin, shoulder-length hair was the color of the mud-stained carpet in the school music room. Teena twirled her hair when she wasn't working, talking, or playing, which was almost all of the time. She'd grab a few strands near her forehead and twirl it around her fingers, and there was a patch on the top of her head where the hair was so thin you could see her scalp, like the spot on a rug at the front of a door where you wipe your shoes before entering the room.

Tay looked disgusted with Teena whenever he noticed her, though mostly he acted as though she didn't exist. Quinn, when he had the occasion to think of Teena, was thankful that she wasn't as obnoxious as a lot of kids. She could even be entertaining, in her own way. She would do her famous apple diver routine at lunch for anyone who'd listen, but if you'd heard it once, you'd heard it all, even if she switched to famous carrot diver or famous potato chip diver. Most of the class thought she was a head case.

Quinn looked back at Sam's paper, which was filled with comic strip frames of skiers falling off of cliffs. Sam began sketching a stingray on skis in the last frame. He paused, lifted his pencil, and sniffed the eraser as Ms. Blakeman and her armload of handouts approached their row. "Aren't you going to write anything?" Sam asked Quinn.

"My grandparents visited us for a week, like they always do, and we played a lot of board games, like we always do," Quinn said. "Who wants to read a paper about that? I sure don't want to write about it."

Ms. Blakeman stopped at Neally's desk. "Your father starts today?"

"Yes, after recess," Neally said. "He can stay until lunchtime, and he says he'd be available to come earlier and correct papers during recess. He'll volunteer every Tuesday, and also Thursdays, if you need him."

"Mmmm." Ms. Blakeman smacked her lips together as if Neally had told her that her father would be bringing a triple-layer, double-chocolate fudge cake to class. "No ifs about that. We'll find plenty of things for him to do. I hope you'll tell him how much I appreciate this, if I forget to say so ten times myself." The teacher sauntered up the aisle toward her desk, happily muttering to herself. "A regular volunteer, oh my!"

8
—
A REGULAR VOLUNTEER

Stormy-without-rain, dry, gusty days when the tall cedars in his front yard whipped back and forth, their spiky branches crackling against one another, were the days Quinn liked the most. The scrawny oak trees that lined the schoolyard's perimeter fences made only a few faint whistles when the wind rustled their wilted leaves; still, any kind of wind-through-the-trees noise made Quinn want to build a campfire and sip hot cocoa. He lost track of time during recess as he wandered about the school, listening to the trees and wondering when the Mistress of Malevolence, aka the playground monitor, would decide it was permissible to run on the field.

Click click, click click.

"Did everyone enjoy recess? Please sit down and listen up!" Ms. Blakeman used her clicker to shoo students to their seats, as if she were herding a flock of lost sheep. "I'd like to introduce someone who's going to be a regular

part of our class. Mr. Bryan Standers will be with us on
Tuesday and Thursday mornings. He'll be working with
our ESL students, and with all of the reading groups on
a rotating basis. He'll also help grade papers, so watch
your handwriting! He's not used to your chicken-scratch
scrawls like I am."

Several students in the front row pretended to be
indignant, which prompted a hearty laugh from Ms.
Blakeman.

Click click, click click.

"We'll find many ways to keep him busy, won't we?!"
Ms. Blakeman's eyes narrowed into slits of delight,
and she turned to Mr. Standers. "Remind me to tell
you about our community service project. Now, fifth
graders, I'm going to ask Mr. Standers to tell you a little
about himself before we get started."

Ms. Blakeman took a step backward, and Bryan
Standers took two steps forward. Neally's father was thin
and tall. His reddish-brown hair curled around his ears
and down the side of his face, blending in with his neatly
trimmed beard and moustache. *He looks like Abraham
Lincoln*, Quinn thought. Quinn snuck his history book
out of his desk and flipped through the pages until he
found Lincoln's picture. Mr. Standers' eyes were as
twinkly as Lincoln's but were lighter in color; also, Mr.
Standers didn't have Lincoln's distinctive, warty knob on
his cheek. He didn't really look like Lincoln at all, Quinn
decided, except for being tall, skinny, and bearded.

"I'm Bryan Standers. It's nice to meet you all." Mr. Standers clasped his hands behind his back and slowly looked around the room, making eye contact with each student. When his eyes met Neally's he blew her a kiss.

"As you may have guessed, I'm Neally's father. And *my* class assignment," he winked at the teacher, "is to tell you about myself. I am married to Ruthanne Maxwell, Neally's mother. We moved here from Spokane, Washington, so that Ruthanne could take a job at Oregon Health Sciences University, where she heads up the nursing recruitment program. I'm a former teacher, currently a stay-home dad. I'm not a scientist, but I love reading science magazines, probably to catch up on what I didn't pay attention to when I was in school. I'm sure none of you diligent students will ever have that problem."

Several students giggled. Mr. Standers looked at Ms. Blakeman, who circled her hands in a "keep going" gesture.

"What else should I tell you?" Mr. Standers thoughtfully stroked his beard. "I like to hike and kayak, and I run and do yoga for exercise. I enjoy cooking and give myself special culinary projects every season. My goal this winter is to learn to make pasta from scratch. I paint with watercolors, mostly landscapes and a few abstracts. Someday I'll get the courage to show my work to ..."

Lily L'Sotho, sitting in the front row between Arturo and Janos, clapped her hands together and squeaked, "Oh!" She covered her mouth and looked down at her desk when she realized her classmates were looking at her.

Mr. Standers smiled at Lily. "Do you like to paint?"

Lily cupped her palms around her cheeks and nodded her head.

"She does indeed," Ms. Blakeman said. "I'm hardly impartial; still, I'd say Lily, and also Arturo and Janos, happen to be three of our class's best artists."

Matt Barker leaned back in his chair. "The worse you talk, the more you get to paint," Matt whispered to Josh.

Josh snorted loudly, then quickly covered his mouth and pretended he was coughing when Ms. Blakeman frowned at him.

"I'm sure we'd all like to see your paintings," Ms. Blakeman said to Neally's father.

"As I was saying, *someday* I'll get the courage to show them to … someone." Bryan Standers lifted his hands and shrugged his shoulders, and several students laughed in recognition and appreciation. It wasn't often that grownups admitted to being embarrassed.

Neally sighed, saying to no one in particular but loud enough for Quinn to hear, "He won't even show them to *me*."

9
THE FIRST TIME I CRACKED MY HEAD OPEN

"I thought he was going to grade papers at lunch."
Sam pointed to a bench by the door to the gym, where
Neally's father and Ms. Blakeman sat. Sam, Quinn,
and Tay sat in a corner of the field, checking out the
GameBox Tay got for Christmas.

"I wonder what they're talking about," Quinn said.

"The community service project," Tay said. "She'll
pass it off on him, that and the ESL kids. You get all
the dumb stuff when you volunteer. You don't see *my*
parents volunteering."

"What did he say that Neally's mom does?" Sam
asked.

"How would I know and why would I care?" Tay
tapped the side of the GameBox. "No way the battery
could be dead already."

"Nursing recruitment," Quinn said. "My mom works with community groups. I heard her tell my dad that nurses are needed to ..."

"Nursing recruitment programs design ways to get people interested in becoming nurses."

The boys looked up to see Neally looking down on them. To Quinn's surprise, Tay held up his GameBox. Neally turned it over in her hand for a moment, said, "Cool," and gave it back to Tay. Tay seemed to have a newfound if grudging respect for Neally. She'd played four square doubles with him at recess, and they'd lasted eight rounds before another team got them out.

"What do your parents do?" Neally asked Quinn. "I know yours," she said to Sam, "are both history teachers."

"Who cares what parents do." Tay punched the reset button on his GameBox. "A thousand points; yes! Bonus round is mine!"

"My mom works for CSO, which is the Community Services Organization. They help people find jobs and housing, doctors, all kinds of things—whatever people need."

"What a great thing to do," Neally said.

"I guess so." Quinn looked around the circle. It felt good to talk about his family. Tay and Sam weren't paying any attention, but at least they weren't interrupting. "Dad's a financial advisor at a bank downtown, the one in the big gray brick building, I forget its name. He tells people what to do with their money. He says he talks to people all day long, which is weird, 'cause he doesn't talk a lot at home."

"Maybe he gets all his words out at work," Neally said.

"Your mom recruits nurses?" Sam asked Neally. "What's up with that?"

"Blah blah blah," Tay droned.

Looking at Sam and Neally, Quinn felt a surge of confidence. "You can leave if we're boring you," he suggested to Tay.

"Maybe he can't leave," Neally said. "Maybe his butt is super-glued to the field."

Sam guffawed. Tay, looking as if he didn't know whether to give Neally a thumbs-up or a noogie, scooted over and made room for her to join their circle.

"Thanks." Neally sat on the ground between Sam and Quinn. "We moved here because of my mom's job. She has a doctorate in nursing."

"A doctor in nursing?" Sam scratched his head.

"Doctor-*ate*," Neally said. "That's a college degree, a much bigger degree than the regular one. She's designing a plan to get more men to go into nursing programs. She's always trying to get my dad to sign up, but after the first time I cracked my head open …"

"The *first* time?" Tay lowered his GameBox.

Quinn glared at Tay and shook his head. Tay loved to hear blood and guts stories, but they made Quinn feel woozy.

"I've done it several times." Neally acted as if she were talking about a no big deal thing, like mixing applesauce with oatmeal. "You get used to the gauze pads. The trick is to use the first-rate kind of gauze to stop the bleeding, not the discount brands with the threads coming off. Cheap gauze sticks to blood when it dries."

Quinn began humming to himself.

"Dad gets dizzy when he sees blood. It's such a joke, my mom thinking my dad could make it through even one day of the first year of nursing school. He'd have to run out of the room during the first minute of Introduction to Scabs."

"Introduction to scabs?!" Tay slapped his thigh. "That's it; *I'm* going to nursing school."

"You have made a positive impression on Mr. Taylor Denton the Third," Sam said. "Congratulations, Ms. Standwell."

"You're welcome. Taylor Denton the ...?"

"The Third," Quinn and Sam chimed in.

"That means there's two more Taylor Dentons?" Neally didn't wait for Tay's reply. "Any clones in your families?" she asked Sam and Quinn.

"Nothin' but clones in mine." Sam grinned.

"You mean clowns," Tay chortled.

"There are red-headed Washingtons in Sam's family

all the way back to infinity," Quinn explained.

"Did you know that the world is full of clones?" Sam asked. "My dad says identical twins are clones. It's not like cloning is anything new in nature. Now, in the Andrews-Lee family ..."

"Andrews-Lee? I like that name," Neally said.

"So does Matt Barker," Tay snickered.

"Yeah, he *loves* my last name." Quinn looked as if he had swallowed a slug. "Matt likes everything about me."

Tay mimicked Matt's voice. "Quinn Andrews-Leeeeeeeeeeeeee!"

"Let me guess: that's supposed to be Matt, teasing someone? How original. Remember," Neally stuck her tongue out, "Thith ith mithier than the thord."

"You might want to try that again," Tay said dryly.

"'The tongue is mightier than the sword.' It's something mom told me, but I looked it up and found out she'd fudged it. It's really, 'The pen is mightier than the sword.' You still get it, right?"

"Right." Quinn smacked his palm to his forehead. "When Matt comes after me with his ninja sword I'll raise my magic ballpoint pen ..."

"Or stick your tongue out," Sam offered.

"And he'll run away, screaming like a kindergartener."

"BRRAAAMP!" Sam mimicked the end-of-recess buzzer. "Mr. Andrews-Lee gets it *not*."

"It means if you practice ... if you learn what to say or not say, you won't have to do the same things Matt does. You won't even want to. You'll find a better way to express, to handle ..." Neally's mouth dropped into a tight line, and she jabbed her fingers in the dirt. "Argh! I can't say it, but I know what I mean." She stood up and swatted the dirt off of the back of her jeans.

10

THE BEST PEANUT BUTTER AND STRAWBERRY JAM SANDWICH EVER

When Ms. Blakeman's class returned from the cafeteria she announced that the special privileges for the-first-day-back-from-vacation would continue: it was buddy lunch day. The students immediately began scooting their desks into semicircles and calling across the room to their friends. Neally's father pulled a chair up to the teacher's desk, and he and Ms. Blakeman began to grade papers.

Quinn asked Tay and Sam to buddy up, but Tay said he was joining Matt and Josh. Sam scooted his desk closer to Quinn's, and invited Neally to do the same.

"Why don't we ask Teena?" Neally suggested.

"What—no!" Sam shushed Neally. "She won't come, anyway. She likes to eat alone."

Neally turned to glance at Teena, who was pulling

plastic bags out of a crumpled paper sack and humming to herself. "Would you two like to come over to my house after school?" Neally asked Quinn and Sam. "I asked my dad; it's okay." Neally reached into her lunch bag and took out a sandwich that looked like a Frisbee cut in half. "I have two Siamese cats, Yin and Yang."

Sam's eyes widened. "My sisters love cats. But we can't have any; my dad's allergic."

"So's my mom," Quinn said. "But her dad used to have a Siamese cat." Quinn pointed at Neally's sandwich. "What's that?"

"Pita bread. See how it opens, like a pocket? You can stuff anything in it." Neally held the sandwich up to her nose. "Dad went for tuna salad today. What was your grandpa's cat named?"

"Jade. She lived to be eighteen, which is old for a cat. After Jade died, Grandma bought a little statue of a Siamese cat. Grandpa put it up on the mantle, next to the other statues."

"What other statues?" Neally asked.

"My grandpa has this really cool collection." Quinn fingered his own peanut butter and strawberry jam sandwich, which seemed dull compared to Neally's. He wondered if she would offer him a bite if he asked to try the pita bread.

"Swap-o-rama!" Sam put half of his turkey and Swiss cheese sandwich on Quinn's desk and took half of Quinn's sandwich. "Tell her about the fat naked guys." Sam crammed almost the entire half of Quinn's sandwich into his mouth.

Neally's raised her eyebrows. "Yes, do tell."

"They're not naked, they're Buddhas." Quinn fake-punched Sam in the shoulder. "Buddhas aren't naked, they just don't wear shirts."

"Only diapers," Sam said, "so you can see their fat naked bellies."

"Loincloths," Quinn insisted. "They wear loincloths."

"Quinn's Grandpa Lee is from China," Sam said to Neally.

"No, my Grandpa Lee's *parents* were from China. I've told you a giga-billion times: Grandpa Lee was born in Ohio."

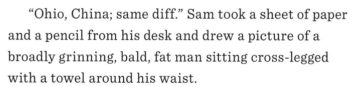

"Ohio, China; same diff." Sam took a sheet of paper and a pencil from his desk and drew a picture of a broadly grinning, bald, fat man sitting cross-legged with a towel around his waist.

"That's the Laughing Buddha!" Neally exclaimed.

"Yeah," Quinn said. "How'd you know that?"

"My parents hang pictures of the world's great

leaders on our living room wall. We've got books about them too. Statues or pictures of the Buddha often show him smiling or laughing. I looked it up, and …"

"Oooooh, Sam's drawing evil devil comics." Matt Barker had crept up behind Sam's desk. "The devil has many disguises," he said, sounding like a Halloween goblin.

"It isn't a devil," Neally said coolly. "Haven't you ever seen a Buddha?"

"If it's not God then it's an idol, or a devil," Matt insisted. "Not only that, it's a fat devil. It's the fattest Satan ever." Matt grabbed Sam's pencil and drew horns on the Buddha's head.

"Horns should taper at the end, be pointier," Sam said. "Like this." Matt gave Sam the pencil, and Sam corrected Matt's additions to his picture.

"Yo, Sam." Matt acted like Quinn and Neally were invisible. "You owe us a buddy lunch. We're gonna play with Tay's new GameBox."

Matt returned to his desk, passing by Teena Freeman, who was spinning her hair with one hand and dancing a carrot stick across her desk with her other hand.

"A hush falls over the crowd as Famous Carrot Diver approaches the ten meter board." Teena spoke barely above a whisper. "Suddenly, in an obvious attempt to influence the judges, Famous Apple Diver insists on going first." Teena walked an apple slice up her arm to her shoulder and dropped the slice into her open carton of milk.

"What a pathetic retard," Matt sneered.

Neally glared at Matt.

"'Scuse me," Matt said. "I mean, what a mentally challenged individual."

"Cut it out, Matt," Quinn mumbled.

"Yeah, I'll cut it out. I'll cut out half my brain and then I'll be like her." Matt pointed at Teena, who was swirling her apple slice in her milk carton and muttering to herself. "You need some filling in," Matt said to Neally. "She's got no father. And her loser mom …"

"Everyone has a father," Neally said.

"Not everyone. Her father is in jail."

"How do you know that?"

"Everyone knows. My dad told my mom." Matt looked over Neally's head, his eyes focusing on the wall behind her. His eyes began to glaze over, and he spoke slowly, as if trying to recall lines he'd had to memorize from a play in the third grade. "Teena's from a single-parent family, which is always bad news for society. Too many kids, and who knows where or who all their fathers are. Her dad's in jail for selling drugs. Her parents did drugs when Teena's mom had her, which is why …" Matt circled his finger by the side of his head. He turned toward his desk, motioning for Sam to follow him.

"I owe Josh two buddy lunches. I promised." Sam looked apologetically at Quinn. "Meet you for some four square at recess?"

Quinn tried to act nonchalant. "Sure."

"I'll see about after school," Sam said to Neally. "I can come over if my homework's done; that's the rule. My sisters will be so jealous when they find out I get to see Siamese cats."

Neally's eyes resembled those of a stalking lion as she watched Sam join Matt and Tay and Josh. "A Buddha is a devil-idol? It should hurt—it should be painful—to be that stupid. If you say something that brainless, the last word out of your mouth should bite your tongue because it's embarrassed to come out. Wouldn't that be awesome?"

Quinn grinned as a vision of Matt Barker's tongue being shredded by a pack of wiener dogs popped into his head. The fantasy faded, and he felt he needed to stick up for his friend.

"Sam's in a Boy Scout troop with Matt and Tay, so he has to get along with Matt. He's doesn't really like Josh, either, but their moms work in the same ..."

"Yes, yes, I get it." Neally loudly bit off the end of a carrot stick. "How long have you known Tay?"

"Since kindergarten. His house is around the corner from ours, and our moms used to walk us to school together."

"So, he's like a habit."

"A habit?" Quinn sat up very straight in his chair.

"He seems kind of ..." The stalking-feline look returned to Neally's eyes. "I just don't see you two as friends."

"Well, we are."

"But Sam is your best friend?"

"That's right." Quinn nodded.

"I don't like the term, 'best friend.' It sounds silly, to rank people that way. But I know that's how other people feel."

"Other people?"

The stalking-cat look disappeared. Neally stared blankly at Quinn, who wondered if Neally realized that she sounded stuck-up.

"What did Matt mean about there being too many kids in Teena's family?" Neally asked.

Quinn looked around the room and leaned closer to Neally. "Like *he* should talk about *other* people having too many kids," he whispered. "Have you seen Matt's mother?"

"Yep. I saw her drop Matt off this morning." Neally held her hands out in front of her, as if she were balancing an enormous beach ball on her stomach.

Quinn quickly glanced toward Matt's desk. "She's always pregnant, and he already has four or five brothers and sisters."

"Five?" Neally gasped. "Plus Matt? No way."

"Way!"

"They're having another?" Neally shuddered. "Don't they know about overpopulation?"

Although Quinn wasn't sure what Neally meant, he assumed it must be wickedly funny. "Yeah, don't they?" he snickered.

"What do Matt's parents do? Wait, I already know his mom's a baby-o-matic. What's up with his dad?"

"God only knows." Quinn nearly choked on his apple. He'd made a clever remark, and wanted Neally to realize that. "His dad's a minister," Quinn explained.

"I get it—nice one!"

"Actually, it's kind of a backwards joke. My mom tells it better: it's not that God knows all about Matt's dad, but Matt's dad knows all about God."

"Oh," Neally said slowly, "now I *really* get it."

"Do you know what Matt said about Lily L'Sotho, after he found out that both her parents are pastors? His dad met Lily's mom and dad at Back to School night. The next day at recess ..." Quinn leaned forward in his chair and lowered his voice. "Matt said his dad told him that Lily's parents aren't real pastors, and their church isn't a real church." Quinn shook his head. "Matt never even talks to Lily, and then the one time he says something about her family, he's mean."

"Matt was mean to someone? Big surprise." Neally yawned. "But why would Matt's dad say Lily's church isn't a real church?"

"I don't know. It isn't *his* church, I guess. Oh yeah, this is even weirder: Matt's dad said that both of Lily's parents can't be the pastors of their church, only Lily's dad can lead their church."

"Wait a second. Matt's dad says he can decide who can be the pastor of someone else's church, the same church that he says isn't a *real* church? Uh huh."

Quinn giggled. "Yeah, that makes a lot of sense."

"Is Lily's mom a pastor?" Neally asked.

Quinn nodded.

"Well then, if she already is one, than she *can* be one. There!" Neally assumed a British accent. "I've run rings 'round him logically!"

"Okay." Quinn scratched his head, "Lily's mom can be a pastor. But not in Matt's church."

"As if anyone would *want* to be a pastor in such a snobby church," Neally sniffed.

"Yeah." Quinn took a bite of his sandwich. It was the best peanut butter and strawberry jam sandwich ever. "As *if*."

11

HOWDY, NEIGHBOR

"Neally Standwell! Neally Standwell!"

Mickey ran to the tetherball court, where Quinn, Sam, and Neally stood in line behind Kelsey King.

"How are you, Neally Standwell?" Mickey gushed.

"I'm very well, thank you, Mickey Andrews-Lee," Neally replied.

"Can you come to our house after school? Can she, Quinn? We have Alice and Peppy—my rat and Quinn's hamster. I have swim practice but not 'til later. We could have snacks and ..."

"I'm going to Neally's house after school," Quinn said.

Neally saw the gray clouds forming in Mickey's eyes, and she turned to Quinn. "Maybe Mickey could ..."

"No way!" Quinn urgently whispered.

Neally silently mouthed *Sorry* to Quinn and then spoke aloud. "As I was going to say, maybe Mickey could show me your pets *after* we stop off at my house?"

"Whoopee!" Mickey raised her arms above her head and pirouetted on one foot, spinning around and around until she staggered backwards, bumping into Sam.

"Perhaps the ballet is not your calling, Mistress Mickey." Sam gently lowered the still-reeling Mickey to the ground.

"My brain is all whirly inside." Mickey tapped her fingers against her temple. "I don't know how dancers can do that without barfing all over their pretty pink tutus."

"YOU'VE DONE YOUR LIMIT," Kelsey yelled to the two sixth graders on the tetherball court. "YOU'RE PLAYING EASIES. LET SOMEONE ELSE HAVE A TURN."

Neally hit the side of her head as if she were trying to dislodge a pebble from her ear.

"She's not really yelling," Sam assured Neally.

"She's not?"

"For anyone else it would be yelling," Sam said. "But for Kelsey, it's just her voice. It's not like she's mad at anything."

"So, does she whisper when she's mad?" Neally asked.

"HOWDY, NEIGHBOR." Kelsey King's mother strutted briskly toward the tetherball line. She waved to Neally in passing and slapped her daughter on the back. "I DROPPED OFF A NOTE AT THE OFFICE," Mrs. King bellowed to Kelsey. "I'M TEACHING A CLASS THIS AFTERNOON, WHICH MEANS YOU'LL BE IN AFTERCARE UNTIL FIVE AND THEN YOUR DAD WILL PICK YOU UP."

"Howdy, neighbor?" Quinn asked Neally. "Does she know you?"

"Our house is across from Kelsey's," Neally explained.

Mickey gazed up in awe at Kelsey's mother and began counting. "One, two, three, four ..."

"Don't point!" Quinn grabbed his sister's finger.

"SEE YA, BABE!" Mrs. King saluted her daughter and marched toward the parking lot.

"You made me lose track!" Mickey whined to Quinn.

"I got up to seven on the left side," Neally said. "You were counting her earrings, right?"

Mickey nodded. "Some of them were so teensy."

"THOSE ARE CALLED POSTS." Kelsey posed triumphantly on the court, holding the tetherball against her hip. "SHE WEARS THE POSTS ON THE LEFT EAR, AND THE HOOPS ON THE RIGHT EAR."

"What does your mom teach?" Neally asked.

"GYMNASTICS. SHE WAS ON THE AMERICAN OLYMPIC SQUAD."

"Why does she wear so many earrings?" Mickey asked.

"WHY NOT?"

Quinn frowned at his sister, but Mickey continued. "Does anyone ever tease her about it?"

"WHAT DO YOU THINK?!" Kelsey cocked her arm back and slammed the tetherball against the pole. "WHICH ONE OF YOU IS GOING TO BE THE FIRST TO DIE?"

12

I KNEW THERE WAS A REASON I LIKED HER

"I bet I can make it all the way home without tripping."
Neally turned around and walked backwards, facing
Sam and Quinn. "Wasn't it cool, at lunch? Like mother,
like daughter."

Sam swung his book pack over his head. "YOU
MUST MEAN THE DEMURE MRS. KING AND HER
MILD-MANNERED OFFSPRING."

"I didn't know you lived so close to school," Quinn
said. "And right across from Kelsey's house; that must
be interesting."

"My parents toured the neighborhood and introduced
themselves after we moved in," Neally said. "They heard
dogs barking, and it got louder when they went from
house to house. But none of our other neighbors have

dogs. Guess where the dogs were? Mom came back in a
really funny mood. She said even the pets have to yell to
be heard in the King household."

"You could do a comic strip about them," Quinn
suggested to Sam.

"Shouting dogs, ah, yes," Sam mused. "Getting their
mouths right would be tricky."

"Dad said it was good to learn that Kelsey was an
only child," Neally said. "He'd assumed the reason she
was so loud was that she was the middle child of seven
kids and had to holler in order to be heard. He said it
was refreshing to have his stereotype busted."

"What's a stereotype?" Quinn asked.

"It's a kind of music system."

"Miz Neally Ray Standwell the First cracks a good
one." Sam stopped at the corner and jingled a key that
hung from a strap around his neck. "This is my street,"
he said to Neally. "I have to write my spelling list so
my sister can check it, then I'll be over. Oh, and do my
piano practice, but that's just twenty minutes. You're on
Greenwood, across from Kelsey's?"

"Yes, the yellow house. See ya later, Sam."

Neally and Quinn continued down the street. "No
homework!" Neally hugged her book pack to her chest.
"I finished it during reading groups. I'm sorry for
inviting your sister without checking with you first. She
really wanted to come over, and I didn't want to leave
her out."

"It's okay."

"I like Mickey. It must be entertaining to have a funny sister, even if she tags along."

"How come you don't have a brother or sister?" Quinn regretted the question as soon as it left his mouth, but Neally didn't act as if she'd been offended.

"I don't know. How come you don't take swimming lessons?"

"I used to. The lessons got boring after a while, for me, anyway, but Mickey loves them. She wants to be in the city swim club. Any kid can join, but you have to try out. Mickey tried out last year." Quinn kicked at a pile of leaves on the sidewalk and grinned with the memory. "She was the youngest kid to try out for the butterfly, which is the most difficult stroke. Mom and Dad and I went to see her. It was so funny; you should have seen it. It took her two minutes—two whole minutes!—to cross the pool after everyone else had finished the race. She just went up and down in the water, staying in the same place, doing that dolphin kick and the big arm circles.

I thought she was drowning at first, but every time her head came up for air she had this big smile on her face. All the adults, even my parents, were trying so hard not to laugh."

"And she still likes to swim?"

"She loves to swim. She's lousy at it, but she loves it, which I don't get. The kid who finished first in the butterfly told her she swam like a spastic snail. She told him she was going to practice all year until her snail legs were strong enough to kick his butt."

"I *knew* there was a reason I liked her. Right face, march!" Neally turned the corner to Greenwood Circle. "I can't wait to find out what my dad thinks about our class. Maybe he'll let you get a preview of your math grade. I wonder how he liked the ESL kids. I wonder why Lily is in ESL. What do you know about her?"

"Not much. I know she doesn't really understand how to play tag. She and her parents moved from Africa, last summer, I think. She's kind of shy—she'll talk a little bit on the playground, mostly with Janos and Arturo, but she almost never speaks in class, even when she's called on during the oral quizzes and you can tell that she knows the answer. But you know what? I love the way she talks."

"I know *exactly* what you mean." Neally ran her fingers over a withered rose bush branch that snaked over a split-rail fence at the front lawn of the

King's house. "Her words are fine, I mean, she uses them correctly, even though sometimes it's hard to understand her. When she talks it sounds like she's singing, even if she's just asking for the bathroom pass. I wonder what country she came from. We could look it up, and—uh oh!" A sharp, raucous yowling started up from the direction of the King's house. "Kelsey's Killer Coyotes sound the alarm," Neally said. "It must be time to cross the street."

13

MUFFINS OF INFINITY

Although Neally had considerately suggested that they save some food for Sam, Quinn was having second thoughts. He had just eaten the best muffin in his life, possibly the best muffin on the planet. He took a sip of milk and eyed the chocolate chip banana muffin Mr. Standers had set aside for Sam.

"Seconds, Quinn?" Mr. Standers held out a plate of still-steaming, fragrant muffins.

"Sure, thanks."

"You're welcome. I'm glad you like them."

"These are …" Quinn licked chocolate off his finger. "These are the muffins of infinity."

"Infinity?" Neally said. "I don't think you're using that correctly. We could look it up."

"I love that word," Quinn said.

"I'm sure infinity means something that never ends, so you wouldn't use it for a …"

Neally's father shook his head.

"Sorry." Neally looked down at her plate, trying to hide her guilty smile.

"Muffins were my culinary adventure project last winter," Mr. Standers said. "My New Year's resolution was to make a different batch every week. Neally started calling me the Muffin Man."

"My mom refuses to make New Year's resolutions," Quinn said. "Dad says that's because the one time she made a resolution she later changed her mind, but she'd already told people what she was going to do and so of course they bugged her about it. I don't know why someone would promise to give up something they love that isn't bad for them, like chocolate."

"So, your mom couldn't swear off the candy bars?" Mr. Standers chuckled. "I don't blame her. But resolutions don't have to be about giving things up. They can be things you vow to start doing, or things you decide to do better. For example, you might resolve to eat healthier or get more exercise."

"Those are typical, boring, adult resolutions," Neally sniffed. "And then there's *my* New Year's resolution. You know what that is, Dad."

"No, can't say I do. Care to refresh my memory?"

"It's to figure out how to stop bone density loss in astronauts."

Mr. Standers placed his hands on his stomach and

laughed heartily. "During Christmas break we watched a lot of videos," he said to Quinn. "The first one was a documentary on the Apollo program. Ruthanne, Neally's mother, decided our holiday video theme should be space travel. We rented everything we could about the subject, and had some interesting discussions about the problems humans face in long-term weightless environments."

"Yeah, I get it," Quinn said nonchalantly. What he got was that Neally's resolution wasn't a wacko statement out of the blue, and that his own half-hearted promise to help his sister clean out her rat's cage every Saturday seemed insignificant by comparison.

"Quinn, eh?" Mr. Standers turned his chair backwards and sat facing the kitchen table, his legs straddling either side of the chair's back. "That's a great name. *The Mighty Quinn.*"

Quinn stared blankly at Neally's father.

"You've never heard that?" Mr. Standers hummed a tune that was unfamiliar to Quinn.

Neally groaned, burying her face in her hands. "All oldies, all the time ... you've got to find another radio station, Dad."

Mr. Standers grinned at his daughter and continued to hum.

"Oh, *that* one," Neally said. "I recognize the tune, but what's it about?"

Mr. Standers shrugged his shoulders. "It's a song from the sixties, so who knows?"

"The Mighty Quinn," Neally said slowly. "That's way cool."

"That's way *not true*," Quinn muttered. "Could you please not say it in class or anything?"

"So, Neally" Mr. Standers said, "you wanted to know about the Three Musketeers?"

"Who?"

"The ESL students in our class: Arturo, Janos, and Lily," Quinn said. "The kids started calling them that because the three of them are always together, but no one ever says it in front of the teachers." He grinned at Neally's father. "How'd you know that name?"

"I didn't, but your teacher did." Mr. Standers ran his fingers through his beard and lowered his voice. "It's scary sometimes, to think of what the grownups are aware of."

"Adults think they know everything," Neally huffed.

"Your Three Musketeers are a great group of kids. *That* should be common knowledge," Mr. Standers said.

"I know Arturo, a little bit. He understands way more English than he speaks. He said he'd teach me to say ..." Quinn felt his face heat up. "He said he'd teach me, uh, some names for someone who acts like a jerk." Quinn covered his eyes and giggled.

"Busted!" Neally exclaimed. "Arturo's going to teach you dirty words in Spanish!"

"No!" Quinn protested. "Not dirty. Just colorful and ... descriptive."

"Young man, do you have enough 'colorful' words for the entire class?" Neally spoke like a substitute teacher with a head cold.

Quinn decided a change in subject was called for. "I'm not sure about Janos. He seems happy enough, but I don't think he's learning a lot. About all he ever says is, 'Duh.'"

"That's 'da.'" Mr. Standers chuckled. "It means 'yes' in his native language, which is a Ukrainian dialect, similar to Russian."

"Janos has the biggest teeth I've ever seen," Quinn said.

"Big, how?" Neally asked. "Big as in their width, or

length? Or quantity?" Neally looked thoughtfully at her father. "How many teeth do people usually have, at our age? We could look it up, in one of Mom's medical books."

"No, Janos' teeth are just big," Quinn said. "You should check 'em out."

"I'll make a note of it," Mr. Standers said. "And yes— or 'da'—it's true that of the Three Musketeers, Janos is having the hardest time learning English. There aren't many resources in this area for foreign languages other than Spanish. Still, he understands more than you might think. And for the life of me, I couldn't figure out why Lily was in the group ..."

"Me too," said Quinn.

"Me three," added Neally.

"Until Ms. Blakeman explained it to me. It's not that Lily doesn't speak English. After my first fifteen minutes with the ESL group I could see that her grammar is better than half the kids in your class. She's in the group to get extra help, mainly to work on her pronunciation. Did you know that Lily can speak at least a little bit of five languages? Some Afrikaans, German, French, a Bantu dialect, *and* English. It's not uncommon for people to speak three or more languages in Namibia, which is where she's from." Mr. Standers ran his fingers around his teacup. "I'd bet there's some interesting stories with Lily's and Janos' families."

"Tay knew you were talking to Ms. Blakeman about the service project during recess," Neally said to her father. "He said that all the dumb projects get passed off to the volunteers. How is that going to work anyway?"

Quinn answered, "Every year all the classes do one and vote for a winner. It's going to be even bigger this year. There's a trophy, and a committee of adults votes for the winner, instead of just the students."

"You're interested in that project, aren't you?"

Quinn felt his face flush under Mr. Standers' attentive gaze. "I guess," he mumbled, slumping in his chair.

"Your friend Tay is partly right, Neally, but it's not dumb. In fact, it sounds interesting and worthwhile to me."

"Me too." Quinn straightened up. Looking into Mr. Standers' eyes was like sinking into the cushions of a comfy couch. Somehow, Neally's dad understood that the project was important to Quinn. No one else cared about the community service project because it was the one project for which there was no pizza party given to the winners. There was no reward for participating, aside from "the respect of our peers," as Matt Barker scornfully put it. Josh, of course, agreed with Matt, but Tay did too, and even Sam. And so Quinn felt like a dork for caring about some stupid class project ...

"... but I do."

"Excuse me?" Neally elbowed Quinn. "You do what?"

Quinn realized he must have spoken out loud.
"Nothing." Quinn glanced at the clock on Neally's
kitchen wall. "If Sam isn't here in ten minutes, can we
take his muffin to Mickey?"

14

THE HAMSTER PATCH QUILT

"Thanks for the bag of muffins." Quinn waved goodbye to Mr. Standers, who stood on his front porch and blew a kiss to his daughter as Neally and Quinn set off for Quinn's house.

"Mickey loves muffins. Mickey loves anything she can chew. She'll be so excited for the treat she might forget about not getting to come to your house and see your cats."

"She can come over next time," Neally said. "She can have Sam's muffin too, if he's a no-show again. What did he say when you called?"

"He said he can't find his piano books, and that he'll meet us later at my house. I didn't know you lived so close; you're just three blocks away." Quinn looked up at the soft, silvery clouds and shifted his book pack to his other shoulder. "Think it's gonna rain?"

"Yep." Neally lifted her hands, as if to push up the sky. "Sooner or later, it always does."

No one responded to Quinn's *I'm home!* when he and Neally opened the front door. "Mom's probably out back. You can leave your jacket here." Quinn dropped his pack on a wooden bench in the entryway. "I'll show you Mickey's room, upstairs. That's where the rodents are."

Neally bounded up the stairs. "I've always wanted a hamster, or a guinea pig. I'd settle for a mouse, but Mom says Yin and Yang would find a way to break into the cage, and the mouse would soon be mincemeat."

It was neither Quinn's hamster nor Mickey's rat that caught Neally's attention when she entered Mickey's room. "Fantabulous!" She pointed to the wall by the closet, where a quilt hung from a wooden rod nailed across the top of the wall. The quilt covered the entire wall, down to the carpet. The quilt's background was a pink cotton cloth, with an overlay pattern composed of a series of interlocking circles made from patches of multicolored fabrics.

"Grandma Andrews, my dad's mom, made it for me before I was born," Quinn said. "See how the circles overlap? That's called a double wedding ring, which is a famous quilt pattern. We call this the Hamster Patch Quilt. Grandma told dad she knew his first child would be a girl ..."

"Ha! What'd I tell you? Adults think they know everything, even when they're wrong."

"... so she made the quilt's background pink."

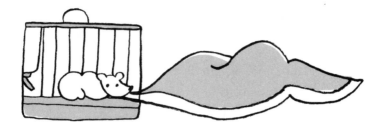

"Why is it the Hamster Patch Quilt? The circles don't look like hamsters."

"I used to keep the cage on a table at the end of my bed. One day, Peppy the First ..."

"The First?"

"All of our hamsters have been named Peppy. It's a tradition. Anyway, I used to have the quilt for a bedspread, and one morning I threw the covers back too far, and Peppy reached through the bars of his cage and got hold of the quilt. When I got home from school, Mom said I had to check out the fanciest hamster nest in the world. A bunch of colored shreds were mixed in with the wood shavings in his cage; Peppy had made his nest from parts of the quilt he'd chewed off! He was so proud of what he'd done. He kept running onto his wheel and then back to his nest, to make sure I saw it."

"You have to be kidding me."

"I kid you not." Quinn pointed to a corner of the quilt where a pink patch of cloth covered a segment where two rings intersected. "Mom made this patch, to fix the part Peppy chewed up."

"The Hamster Patch Quilt," Neally murmured. She ran her hand over the small pink patch. "It's even cooler this way than if it was whole and perfect, because now there's a story about it."

"I know." Quinn grinned so hard his face ached. "I *love* that story."

"It's a fantabulous quilt," Neally said. "It's a quilt … for all infinity."

Quinn's eyes widened.

"Infinity *is* a great word." Neally smiled saucily. "But if your grandma made the quilt for you, why is it in Mickey's room?"

"Grandma made quilts for all her grandkids, but she died before Mickey was born."

"So you gave your quilt to Mickey? That was nice of you."

"Well, it's pink."

"Well, duh. Do you like it?"

"Sure. It's a great quilt."

"It's just a color, you know," Neally said. "I don't care for pink, either—I'm more into dark colors, like green and purple. But it's not like colors can zap your chromosomes. I don't understand why some boys act like they're afraid of pink."

"I'm not afraid of pink. If I was, I'd be afraid of Alice's eyes." Quinn pointed at the rat cage.

"Yes!" Neally reached for the cage door. "I can hold her, right?"

"Sure. She won't bite."

"My mom hates rats," Neally said gleefully. "She says their tails look like freeze-dried snakes. Hey Alice, your whiskers tickle my hands!" Alice crawled up Neally's arm and perched on her shoulder. "Yin and Yang would really go for her. For a midnight snack, I mean. I'm sorry my dad wouldn't let me wake them when we were at my place. Afternoon is their nap time."

"That's okay. They were awesome just to look at." Quinn let Alice sniff his finger. "Siamese are the best cats."

"They're not pure Siamese, which is a good thing, because they don't have those creepy meows that sound like someone's pinching a howler monkey," Neally said. "Mom says they've got just enough Siamese in them to make them too smart for their own good. They can open drawers, and even the front door screen. Sometimes Yin drags the newspaper to the back porch in the morning, and then Yang shreds it."

"If you want a pet to fetch the paper, you need a dog." Quinn put Alice back in her cage.

"Who wants to teach anything to fetch?" Neally asked.

Quinn turned his attention to the hamster cage. "I wish we had a dog. I'd like a big one, an Irish setter or an Alaskan husky, not a little yippy dog." He stuck his finger through the bars and spun the wheel. "Have you ever had a dog?"

"We had a chocolate Lab puppy. He was cute, but dumb as a box of crayons. He'd get loose and run out into the street and chase passing cars." The muscles in Neally's face curved as if she was telling a joke, but her voice was small and serious. "Then, one day, he caught one."

"Oh."

"I think Dad would like for us to have another dog. He loves all kinds of animals. But Mom doesn't care for dogs. They grovel, you know."

"Grovel?"

"It's like begging. Dogs do whatever you want, because they want you to be nice to them. It's so ... *desperate*. Kind of like Tay. Mom says she doesn't respect people who grovel, so why would she want that in an animal? Hey, is Mickey outside with your mom?"

"Probably." Quinn looked out the window, and indeed, Mickey and his mother were weeding the ground by the azalea plants. "What do you mean, 'like Tay?' About the groveling stuff."

"Sorry." Neally sounded anything but sorry. "I've noticed how Tay acts tough with you and Sam, then he's all loose and wiggly when Matt is around. It's obvious he wants Matt to like him."

"So?" Quinn turned from the window. "Let's go downstairs."

"So ..." Neally paused. "I guess it *would* make anyone's

life easier, to have Matt like them."

"Tay's having a sleepover at his house on Friday. Sam's going too." Quinn stopped at the top of the stairway, and Neally almost bumped into his back. "Last year Sam's dad said that Tay was a 'fair-weather friend.' Sam's dad likes the weather, but I don't think that was a compliment."

"Will Matt be at the sleepover?"

"Tay had to invite Matt. His parents made him invite his entire Scout troop." Quinn lowered his eyes, as if speaking to his shoes. "I'm invited, but I don't know if I'll go. I've never done a sleepover all the way. I tried a few times at Sam's, but I had to call my dad to come get me. I can't sleep at sleepovers. There's too much noise, and ..."

And Quinn missed sleeping in his own bed, but he wasn't going to tell Neally that. He missed the way his blankets smelled, like the flowers his mother planted by the back fence. He missed the sound of the hamster wheel spinning in Mickey's room. He missed knowing his parents were down the hall and would wake up if the house caught on fire. He even missed his sister's snoring—a wheezy, chuckling sound, as if she were giggling in her sleep.

"Sleepovers are *over*, all right," Neally declared. "*Over*-rated, if you ask me. I'll show you a yoga breathing trick my dad taught me. I use it whenever I need to calm down or have trouble sleeping. Did I tell you the idea my dad has for the community service project?"

"Only about ten times while your dad was bagging the leftover muffins for us."

"We'll get to spend a day outside, digging in the mud. I'll wait until Sam gets here to tell the details—oh, hold on, idea alert! Let's put the muffins out with glasses of milk and act like we don't know where they came from. We'll tell Mickey that the muffin fairy visited your house."

15

THE MUFFIN FAIRY

"Pa, did Ma tell you what happened?" Mickey waved her fork as if it were a magic wand. "We got visited by the muffin fairy!"

"The muffin fairy?" Mr. Andrews asked.

"Uh, Mickey? Pa? *Ma*?" Quinn looked across the table and tapped his fork against the side of his head.

"We've been reading *Little House on the Prairie*," Ms. Lee explained. She passed a platter of potato pancakes to her husband. "Try one topped with applesauce. I think it's even better than with sour cream."

Mickey's eyes widened. "'Scuse me." She dashed into the kitchen and returned to the table, clutching a vial of green food coloring. "We do the funnest art projects at school. Watch." She reached for the bowl. "I can turn applesauce into diarrhea."

"Mic-*key*!" Jim Andrews whisked the vial from his daughter's hand.

"Gross!" Quinn dropped his fork. "That's potty talk. She has to leave the table, right?"

"Diarrhea is not potty," Mickey huffed. "It's more like ..."

"Time out!" Marion Lee lowered her head to the table. "Someone, anyone, start a new subject, *please*."

Mr. Andrews took the food coloring and the applesauce to the kitchen counter. He returned to the table with a bowl of sour cream. "Who here knows of any school subjects suitable for dinner conversation?"

"I got one." Quinn's knees pumped enthusiastically under the table. "Mr. Standers has an idea for our class service project."

"Mr. Standers, he's Neally's father." Ms. Lee raised her head from the table. "Neally came over this afternoon," she said to her husband. "She, and then Sam, and then the muffin fairy."

"The muffin fairy?" Mr. Andrews looked confused.

"Ya shoulda had a muffin, Pa." Mickey clasped her hands together. "It was taste bud rodeo!"

"The class project is going to be awesome," Quinn said. "Neally told Sam and me ..."

"And me!" Mickey said.

"You were just at the table, Neally was talking to me and Sam. And you have to promise," Quinn jabbed his finger at Mickey, "not to copy our idea. Your class has to do your own project." Quinn looked at his parents. "You know the Noble Woods?"

"I love that park." Ms. Lee patted her husband's knee. "We haven't been there in months."

"I'm still wondering about muffins and fairies," Mr. Andrews said. "Where did ..."

"Actually, Mom, it's a nature preserve," Quinn said, "which is different than a park. Mr. Standers got the idea from when he and Neally went to OMSA and saw the Northwest Habitats exhibit. Our class will do trail work and habitat restoration, which means cleaning up ..." Quinn bit his lip, trying to remember what Neally had said. "Where there's been damage by human activity."

"That certainly sounds worthwhile," Ms. Lee said.

"The project judges go for stuff like that—worthwhile stuff. And Ms. Blakeman loves the idea. Neally's dad checked out the city's website. Habitat restoration is a regular city works project, but it was cancelled this year 'cause there's not enough money. We'll do it and save the taxpayers' money! I just know we're going to win first prize. Not that that's why we're doing it," Quinn quickly added.

"I got lost in the woods back there," Mr. Andrews said. "What's OMSA?"

"It's that museum in Portland," Ms. Lee said. "Oregon Museum of Science and something."

"And Arts," Quinn said. "Neally's family just moved here, and they're members already."

"Didn't your class have a field trip to OMSA?" Ms. Lee asked.

"That was last year, and we didn't stay very long. We only had enough time to see the human development exhibit. The childbirth part was boring or yucky, I couldn't decide which one."

"Yucky gets my vote," Ms. Lee said.

"Neally says the chemistry lab is ultra cool. It has information on DNA and chromosomes. She used that word twice today, and you don't usually hear it even once a day."

"She said ultra cool two times?" Mickey said.

"No, *chromosomes*. But, we were arguing about colors." Quinn frowned. "I don't think she knew what she was talking about."

"Then ask her," Ms. Lee suggested.

"She'd probably act like she does know, even if she doesn't. She'd say she looked it up. She always says that."

"She is a clever one," Ms. Lee said. "What are Neally's parents like? I know her father can bake a mean muffin."

"Now we're getting somewhere," Mr. Andrews muttered.

Mickey wiggled in her seat. "Her dad is the muffin fairy?"

"I don't know her mom yet," Quinn said. "She's a nurse. I saw her once, at school. She looked nice. Neally's dad, well, I think he's a lot like Neally. Or maybe Neally's like him. That's why she's ... ah, foof! It's hard to explain."

"Quinn went to Neally's after school," Ms. Lee said to her husband. "What is Neally's home like?" she asked Quinn.

"The walls in their house are covered with books." Quinn arranged the potato pancakes on his plate, leaning them against one another as if he were making a teepee. "There's a bookcase against every wall. Every room is like a different library. Neally and her dad played this game with me, to see if I could figure out the subjects, and I could, mostly. The living room has travel books on one side and also some biographies. On the other side are books on religion and ... the subject that's about thinking about the meaning of life."

"Philosophy?" Quinn's mother offered.

"Yeah, philosophy. And in the kitchen, well, that was easy. Books on cooking and eating. You know, food stuff."

"Who needs books on eating?" Mickey asked. "Everyone knows how to eat."

"In the hall there's dictionaries and maps on one side, foreign languages on the other ..."

"Ah, the reference section," Mr. Andrews said.

"... and history. And a whole bookcase for Neally's mom's medical books. There's even books in the garage, about gardening and plants. Their house is kinda small ..."

"Or perhaps it just seems that way, with all the literary clutter," Mr. Andrews said.

"They only have a one-car garage, which is okay since they only have one car. But they have to park it in the driveway 'cause the garage is full of stuff: more books, wood and metal parts, tools, bikes, and two kayaks! Neally's dad bought them at a kayak rental shop sale. He buys everything used. Neally says his motto is 'Reduce, reuse, recycle.'"

"Hear! Hear!" Marion Lee raised her water glass. "We should all live by those wise words."

Mr. Andrews raised his glass and smiled through clenched teeth. "I'd be out of a job if everyone lived by those words."

"It's not fair." Mickey slumped in her chair. "I didn't get to go to Neally's house." She sat up straight, folded her hands on the table, and said brightly, "But Neally said I could go next time."

"You won't like it," Quinn teased. "They almost don't have a TV."

"How can you almost not have a TV?" Ms. Lee asked.

"They have one, but it's so small it's practically not worth it. I asked Neally about it, and ..."

"Don't tell me you made rude comments about the size of their television set, or about anything in their home?"

"Mo-om! I'm not that clueless. Besides, you can't be rude to Neally. She won't take it that way. When I said I thought it was interesting—the smallest TV ever is interesting, right? You know what she said?"

"I bet she said it like this." Mickey lifted her chin and pretended to toss back her hair. "I love it when she does that."

"You know, Mickey, your hero Neally never interrupts me," Quinn said.

"Oh yes, she does," Mickey insisted. "She does it a *lot*."

Mickey was right. But no way was Quinn going to admit it to his parents. "I asked about her small TV and these were her exact words: 'It's not like having a bigger screen makes the shows any better, or you any smarter for watching them.'"

Ms. Lee raised her glass again. "I'm starting to like this girl even more."

"Me too," said Mr. Andrews.

"Me three," said Mickey. "And Sam and Quinn makes me four and me five."

"I gather you and Neally and Sam are hanging out together," Ms. Lee said. "But Sam didn't go over to Neally's?"

"We waited but he never showed up, so I called him. He couldn't find his piano book. His sister's in charge ..."

"Yea!" Mickey clapped her hands.

"His *older* sister," Quinn grimaced at Mickey, "is in charge after school, and she wouldn't let him go 'til he'd done his practice. So he pretended to find his book and faked a practice and met us over here. Neally's dad packed up the leftover muffins for him ..."

"And for me!" Mickey exulted. "Muffin fairy, muffin fairy!" She poked Quinn in the ribs.

Quinn's father leaned back and folded his hands across his stomach. "Patience is its own reward," he said. "If you listen long enough, most conversations will eventually make sense."

"What did you do at Neally's house?" Ms. Lee asked.

"We ..." Quinn was going to talk about Neally's cats, but thought better of it. Mickey seemed thrilled to have discovered the identity of the muffin fairies, and he didn't want to hear about how unfair it was that he'd gotten to see Siamese cats. "We waited for Sam, and Neally showed me her mom's medical books. There are entire books about the awful things that can happen to human bodies. Neally showed me her favorite, the one about skin diseases and injuries." Quinn closed his eyes and recited slowly. "Der-ma-toe-log-ick something. It's got pictures of cuts, rashes, bites, and bruises, you name it, plus boils and sores and even infected amputations! The oozing ones are way intense."

"Lovely." Quinn's mother forced a smile. "Can you imagine posing for those pictures?"

"Neally said patients let doctors take the pictures, to help people learn how to treat injuries and diseases. They take pictures of the cut or whatever at the beginning, and later they take more pictures to show how it heals. They don't show faces unless the rash or cut is on the face; it's mostly body stuff. It's cool to look at, but I don't think I'd let a doctor take a picture of *my* scabs."

"I would." Mickey lifted her scraped elbow above her head. "Say cheese!"

16
—

WITH LIBERTY
AND JUSTICE
FOR ALL

"Did you survive the weekend?"

Quinn twisted in his chair and shot a *Huh?* look at Neally.

"You know." Neally closed her eyes, laid her head on her desk, and pretended to snore.

"Sure." Quinn was mildly annoyed that Neally would ask him about the sleepover, what with her desk being right next to Tay's. But Tay was frantically rummaging through his book pack and seemed unaware of the world beyond his desk.

"No way the math packet is due today," Tay muttered. "No way."

Quinn looked around. Everyone was seated, except for Josh, Matt, Teena, and Lily, who were hanging up their coats in the back. He scribbled a note and tossed it on Neally's desk.

Matt & Josh & Brandon and another scout stayed home sick! We were up 'til midnight playing Risk! I even got to sleep! Slow deep breaths, you know!

Neally clasped her hands over her head like a prizefighter. "Yes!" she exulted. "Victory to the Mighty Quinn!"

"The Mighty Quinn?" Tay looked up from his book pack.

"Math worksheets were due last *Friday*, Tay," Neally said. "But just the first two pages."

Click click, click click.

"Okay fifth graders, it's Monday." Ms. Blakeman's students stood up and faced the flag that hung from a pole bolted to the top of the chalkboard.

I pledge allegiance ...

Teena placed her right hand over her heart, twirled her hair with her left hand, and inched toward her desk.

... of the United States of America ...

Josh elbowed Matt and pointed at the last row, toward Tay, Neally, and Teena. "Listen," Josh whispered.

Tay amused himself by using an up-tone on every

other word: ... *and* **to** *the* **republic** *for* **which** *it* **stands** ...
Teena hummed to herself, occasionally joining in the
pledge but missing most of the words. Neally stood tall
and silent, facing the front of the room, her hands at
her side.

... with liberty and justice for all.

Click click, click click.

"Seats, everyone. Arturo, would you please help
me with these?" Ms. Blakeman and Arturo began to
distribute a handout. "The first page is a description of
the Noble Woods Preserve, the site of our community
service project. The second page is the formal
description of the project that goes to the judges. The
third page lists what you'll need to take on the trip. Mr.
Standers and I will provide the tools; you'll need boots,
gloves, clothes that can get dirty ... it's all there, on page
three. The last page is the permission slip. We'll be there
through lunchtime, so everyone will need to pack a lunch
that day."

Ms. Blakeman dropped a handout on the floor, and
her glasses slipped off the end of her nose when she
leaned over to retrieve the papers. "I need a speed
bump," she said, tapping the end of her nose. "Our bus
will leave promptly at eight-thirty and be back in the
early afternoon. The trip is not until next month, but we
need a head count for ..."

"One, two, three ..." Sam pointed at the desks in front
of him. "Where's Brandon's head?"

"… so please have the permission slip back by Friday."

"Forty acres of hiking trails, bridges, and overlooks … blah blah blah." Sam read from the handout. "Creeks meandering through natural forests and meadows, set aside to preserve native vegetation." Sam lowered the handout and used his Serious Voice. "It's a good thing for young people to help preserve native creek meandering."

"A field trip in February," Tay said glumly. "It'll rain, for sure."

"You are likely correct, Master Denton," Sam said. "My dad could give us the forecast."

"YOO HOO!" Kelsey flapped her hand and spoke before Ms. Blakeman called on her. "HOW MANY ADULT VOLUNTEERS DO YOU NEED? MY MOM COULD GO, AND …"

"We're not kindergartners." Josh looked down the row of desks and winked at Matt. "We don't need someone to hold us by the hand in case we need to go to the toity in the woods."

Although the entire classroom erupted with hilarity, Josh's bizarre honking was easily recognizable above the rest of the students' laughter.

"Spring is early this year," Neally said. "I hear geese returning from their winter migration."

Click click, click click.

Ms. Blakeman wrote Josh's name on the chalkboard.

"Five minutes off recess," she said to Josh, "for speaking out of turn. Fifth graders, while Josh could have chosen better words to express his opinion, it's true, you're no longer in kindergarten, and I expect your behavior shall demonstrate that fact. At the preserve we'll divide into three groups, with one adult supervisor per group. Mr. Standers and I will each lead a group ..."

Please, please, not Kelsey's mother. Quinn focused his thoughts, wondering if it was possible to send a telepathic message to his teacher. Kelsey waved her hand and wriggled in her chair, trying to restrain herself until she was called upon. Her cheeks began to turn red.

"Warning, warning," Sam said. "Evacuate deck three; containment breach imminent."

"Call on her before she explodes," Tay muttered.

"I appreciate your offer, Kelsey," Ms. Blakeman said. "Your mother is a champion field trip leader, and I'm sure we'll use her skills later in the year. But we're going to give other parents the chance to participate. Mrs. L'Sotho, Lily's mother, will be our third group leader."

Kelsey's hand thudded onto her desk. Quinn realized he had been holding his breath. He exhaled slowly, savoring the smile he could feel spreading across his face.

Victory to The Mighty Quinn.

17

COULD SHE BELCH THE ENTIRE PLEDGE OF ALLEGIANCE?

BRRAAAUUMPPPH.

Quinn cupped his hand over his mouth and mumbled "Excuse me" to the other kids in the four square line. It was nice of Neally to have shared her sandwich with him, but the pita's garbanzo bean filling was coming back to haunt him.

Tay, always appreciative of a good belch, raised his hand and batted an imaginary high-five to Quinn. "You are the *man!*"

"Quinn may be the man," Neally laughed, "but who goosed that water buffalo?" She shuddered and palm-smacked the side of her head.

Every kid standing in the four square line laughed. It was good laughter, Quinn thought, even if Matt joined in, because everyone acted as if Quinn had produced that splendid burp on purpose, solely for their amusement.

"You gotta meet my Aunt Gwen." Matt ran his fingers over his forehead, twisting his pale eyebrow hairs into little spikes. "If you give her a soda pop she can burp the alphabet."

"The entire alphabet?" Neally asked.

"A to Z."

Matt pulled his shoulders back, looking tall—well, tall for Matt—and proud. For the first time in a long time Quinn didn't feel a knot in his chest at the sound of Matt's voice. And so for the first time in a long time Quinn asked Matt a question. Giving Matt an opportunity to open his mouth was usually the last thing on Quinn's mind.

"Can your aunt do that with any kind of drink?"

"No, it has to be carbonated. There's a trick to it." Matt spoke earnestly, as if he were describing how to decipher a treasure map. "And not all sodas are created equal; you gotta test out the brands. Orange soda, no way. A total dud."

BREEAPEEEE DARRROOOOOP!

All eyes turned to Josh, who looked breathless but proud after his enormous burp.

"Dude!" Tay said admirably.

"Did you hear it—'Beavers drool?' I burped, 'Beavers drool,'" Josh insisted.

"The Beavers are the Oregon State University's mascot," Sam whispered to Neally. "My mom went to OSU."

"Then you're a Beavers fan?" Neally whispered back.

Sam glanced at Matt and Tay. "Sometimes."

"Does this mean you drool?"

"Lemon-lime sodas are okay and colas are better, but not the diet kind." Matt continued to earnestly explain the finer points of burp fabrication. "Aunt Gwen says root beer's best. She can do the whole alphabet, plus punctuation, on two gulps of A & W Classic Recipe. She's practicing the U of O fight song."

"That's the University of Oregon," Sam explained to Neally.

"Ducks rule!" Tay solemnly announced.

A light flashed in Neally's eyes. "*That's* the duck school?"

"U of O, The Fighting Ducks," Matt said. "They rule."

Neally splayed her knees out and waddled from side to side. "I rule!" she quacked.

The four square server yelled "Next!" and bounced the ball to Tay. Tay dribbled the ball but did not join the game.

"Imagine being able to belch the Pledge of Allegiance," Tay mused. "That would be the best skill ever. You'd be remembered for all of school history."

"I would pay real money to be able to do that," Josh chimed in.

"It would be a most admirable talent, but the pledge is longer than the alphabet," Sam pointed out. "It might take four gulps of industrial strength root beer."

"I agree, it would be a worthy contribution to our school's culture. Does your aunt enjoy a challenge?" Neally elbowed Matt. "Could she belch the entire Pledge of Allegiance?"

Matt nodded his head. "Piece of cake."

"I was asking about the pledge." Neally laughed. "But she could burp cake if she liked, I wouldn't mind."

"At least she'd be saying the pledge," Matt said. "Which is more than some people do."

"I said, *next!*" the four square server called out.

Tay bounced the ball to Josh and turned his back to the four square court. Josh threw the ball back to the server and looked at Matt and Neally. "This'll be way better than any bouncy-bouncy ball game," Josh muttered, crossing his arms in front of his chest.

"Respect alert, respect alert." Sam spoke in his robot voice. "Pledge-belcher; must alert proper authorities."

Neally returned Matt's stare, but said nothing.

"Like I said, even belching the pledge would at least be saying it," Matt said. "Which is more than some people do."

Although Quinn was certain there was an accusation behind Matt's words, the usual, *I'll-get-you* look in Matt's eyes was absent. Matt seemed more curious than angry.

Quinn wasn't sure if that realization made him feel relieved or anxious.

"Some people? Some people?" Sam mechanically lifted and lowered his arms. "Does not compute."

"Well?" Matt said.

"Well, a deep subject," Neally replied. "Or sometimes, it's just a hole in the ground."

"So, why don't you say it?"

"Why doesn't she say what?" Quinn asked.

"The Pledge of Allegiance," Josh said. "We heard her, right Matt? She didn't say it."

"You heard me *not* say it?" Neally asked. "What is it you heard me say, if I didn't say it?"

"We ... ah ..." Josh's brow scrunched and his lips twitched.

"Uh-oh, Josh is trying to think," Sam whispered to Quinn. "Better fetch the drool bucket."

"Nothing." Matt's voice was oddly calm. "She said nothing. That's the point. Everyone else was saying the pledge."

"You didn't say the pledge?" Sam asked.

"Didn't." Neally nodded her head. "Don't."

"Why don't you say the Pledge of Allegiance?" Matt asked.

"I used to. One day I thought about it, and so now I don't."

"Why don't you say the pledge?" Matt persisted.

"Why do you care?"

"We say the pledge in class every Monday," Matt said. "That's what we do."

"I don't try to get anyone else *not* to say it, so why should anyone care if I do or don't?"

"Because we're supposed to say it, as a class. It's to show we're all together, to support our country. It's important."

Matt did not sound angry, more like confused, Quinn thought. Still, Quinn began to feel the familiar, *look-out-Matt-is-talking* tightness clasping at his stomach.

Neally smiled sweetly. "If it's important to a person, shouldn't that person be thinking about what he's saying, instead of eavesdropping on other people?"

Quinn counted eight silent seconds before Matt responded.

"Maybe you don't support our country." The cold, biting edge had returned to Matt's voice. "Maybe you don't love our country."

Josh quivered in anticipation of the chance to mock someone. "Maybe she's a fat-Buddha-statue lover, like Quinn's grandpa."

"What?!" Quinn sputtered. "My grandpa's not ..."

"A fat Buddha? How redundant." Neally patted Josh's shoulder, as if calming a hyperactive poodle she was trying to paper-train. "Translation, Josh: redundant is the ultimate 'duh.' When have you ever seen a skinny Buddha?"

"Bud-*duh*!" Tay said. "Excellent."

"So, Neally, why don't you say the pledge?" Sam looked around at the other kids, his eyes composed and curious. "I'm just asking. I don't care if you do or not. But if you were, say, from another country, where they don't ..."

"She's from Washington state, not another country," Matt persisted.

"Or maybe some kind of different religion?" Sam offered.

"Yaweh's Disciples?"

The group turned in unison to look toward the musical voice that floated up from the end of the line. No one had noticed that Lily L'Sotho had joined the four square line. Lily looked startled by all the eyes trained upon her, and for a moment it seemed that she might bolt like a deer and run for the trees.

"Huh?" Josh looked around the schoolyard. "Where's Arturo? Where's Janos?"

"Zip it." Tay crooked his arm, as if he were going to put a headlock around Josh's mouth.

Lily's chin dipped, and she fingered the hem of her skirt and did not make eye contact with the others as she spoke. "There are people who take no oaths." She paused, searching for the right words. "Their faith says make no pledge, only to their god."

"I've read about that," Neally said. "There are groups like the Yaweh's Disciples ..."

"Oh yeah, Joey's disciples," Josh said. "What kind of church would ...?"

"It's pronounced YAW-weigh," Neally said. "*Yaweh's* Disciples. Is that your parents' church, Lily?"

"No." Lily smiled bashfully at Neally. "My family, we are not them."

"Oh, *those people*." Tay grimaced. "They go from house to house and knock on your door. They try to get you to invite them inside, and you don't even know them."

"Why would anyone want to talk with someone they don't know?" Quinn asked.

"Salespeople talk to people they don't know all the time," Sam said. "Ever done a fundraiser for soccer or Scouts?"

Quinn shot a dirty look at Sam, who knew full well that Quinn was not a Scout and had never been on a sports team.

"We've had them come to our street," Sam said. "People from other churches too. If my sister sees them coming she pulls down the window shades and says we can't answer the door."

"They say they're not selling anything," Tay said. "But my mom says they try to get you to buy their magazine that says their church is right and yours is wrong."

"*They're* the ones who need something that tells the

truth," Matt said. "If they came to our house, my dad would set them straight in no time."

"That would be so much fun to watch!" Neally clapped her hands. "Like those wrestling matches on TV!"

"*You* watch wrestling?" Sam laughed.

"No. But I've read about it. My parents say we're not sophisticated enough for such ..." Neally held her fingers up in the quotation sign, "'high class entertainment.' But I bet they'd let me watch '*My God Can Head Slam Your God.*'"

"There's only one God." Matt clenched and unclenched his fists. "You shouldn't make fun about stuff like that."

"Shouldn't?" Neally flipped her hair off her shoulders. "One person shouldn't tell another person what to talk about."

"This is so boring," Tay yawned.

"God is *not* boring." Matt's face turned the color of Ms. Blakeman's chalk.

"Look, no one's on the court anymore—we even bored the server out of the game." Tay gestured toward the empty four square court. "Why is anyone talking about this stuff; who cares? Does this look like a church?"

"It sure doesn't look like a four square game," Sam piped up.

"Superb point, Mr. Washington," Neally said.

"C'mon, we'll double up, everyone can play. Lily, would you be in my square? You and I could beat 'em all, standing on one leg." Neally raised her foot and hopped toward Lily.

Quinn ran to the server's square with Sam. "Quick," he called back to the others, "before the sixth graders come back."

Sam bounced the ball toward the students standing in line. Matt swung his foot, as if to kick the ball, and Neally tripped over his shin and fell face-first to the blacktop. When she lifted her head, two bright scarlet rivulets streamed from her nose.

Quinn felt as if everything soft and liquid was draining from his head. He ran to Neally; the other kids froze for a moment, as if they'd been planted in the blacktop. Quinn saw from their expressions that he wasn't the only one who knew exactly what had just happened.

"Whoa!" Matt stepped in front of Quinn. "Watch where you're going. You okay?" Matt reached out to Neally, who ignored his outstretched arm and tried to stand up on her own. She staggered, reached out to steady herself and grabbed Matt's arm, accidentally pushing up the sleeve of his jersey.

"Uh!" Matt flinched.

Neally saw a large, purple-green bruise on Matt's forearm. She pulled her hand back, and Matt quickly pushed his sleeve back down.

"Tay, help me get some wet paper towels." Matt began issuing orders. "Sam, Josh, go get the school nurse, what's her name?"

"Nurse Parker," Sam said.

"No, it's okay," Neally protested, "I'll be fi— *bleeackkkk*." Neally spit out a clot of blood that had dripped into her mouth.

The boys ran off on their rescue errands. "Help, someone help us," Lily whispered, as she anxiously looked around the schoolyard. She fumbled through her skirt pocket and found a wad of tissues, which she handed to Neally. "Be like this." She tilted her head back, indicating to Neally to do the same. "I will go for help, for Ms. Barnes." Lily ran off in search of the playground supervisor.

"Ms. Barnes, that'll be a big help ... *acck gack*." Coughing and spluttering, Neally lowered herself to the blacktop and pressed the blood-soaked tissues against her nostrils. "She'll blast her whistle, and my nose will be too scared to bleed."

Quinn sat down beside Neally. As long as he could hear her talk and not have to look at her nose, he knew she'd be all right. He knew *he'd* be all right.

"Are you really okay?" he asked.

"I'm a little dizzy … It's just a bloody nose, and not even my first. But did you see *that*?"

"I know." Quinn shook his head in disgust. "Matt tripped you on purpose."

"No, not that. I mean when I grabbed his arm—that huge bruise on Matt's arm. Where'd he get a bruise like that?"

"He's a sports jock," Quinn said. "Haven't you heard to the nth time that his soccer team is going to the league finals?"

"Soccer players get bruises on their shins, not their arms," Neally insisted.

"And their legs, sometimes. On the top part."

Quinn and Neally looked up at the sound of Teena's spacey voice. Where did she come from? Quinn wondered. He was certain he hadn't seen her standing in the four square line.

"*Ack*; yucko." Neally cleared her throat. "I swallowed some of this gunk. Excuse me." She spit a bloody wad into the tissues.

Quinn rummaged through his pockets, but found no tissue. Teena reached into her own jacket pocket, removed a piece of a crumpled cafeteria napkin and gave it to Neally.

"Thanks, Teena," Neally said.

"Uh-hum," Teena mumbled.

"Are you going to tell on Matt?" Quinn asked Neally.

"Why bother?" Neally slowly pushed herself to her feet.

"You should tell."

"You said it before," Neally said. "Matt never does anything when a grownup is looking, so it's my word against his."

"Not just yours—I saw it. So did everyone." Quinn glanced at Teena. "I'd tell the truth."

Teena turned around and walked a zigzag line toward the tetherball courts, spinning her hair and humming the *There was an old lady who swallowed a fly* song.

"Okay, so we'll need a more reliable witness." Quinn sighed. "She's such a … lurker. You don't even notice her, and then she's just *there*."

Neally put her hand on Quinn's shoulder. Neally was always touching people, putting her hand on your elbow or patting your arm, in a nice or joking way. But this time Quinn felt like crying when he looked at her. She radiated gratitude, but there was another mood, something else that seemed so out of place in those typically indomitable, cosmic green eyes: resignation.

"I'm sure about *you*. About you telling the truth. But are you sure about everyone else?"

"You're not going to tell anyone?" Quinn knew the

answer to his question, and wondered why he bothered asking it. "Someone has to; Neally, oh, c'mon. You have to tell."

Neally shook her head. "Look, even if we report him and we both know it's him ... argh! Don't you get it? There we'd be, maybe three of us instead of just him and me, but he'd still think he'd won, because he got us there, with him. Besides, the principal would probably make all of us go to those conflict management sessions after school, which are so lame."

SSSSSSSQQQQQQQQQUUUUUUURRRRRK!

Sam, Lily, and the school nurse ran toward the four square court. Ms. Barnes marched thirty feet behind them, swinging her arms forcefully, her whistle clenched between her teeth. "Slow down, all of you! That goes for you too, Annie Parker!"

Nurse Parker glanced back in astonishment but did not slow her pace. Ms. Barnes continued to yell. "Y'all think you're going to help by tripping and bloodying *your own* noses?!"

"Here comes Rescue 9-1-1," Quinn said. "I feel safer already."

"Nice one. Think I ought to go for it? After all, they went to so much trouble. Ooo-wooooh." Neally clutched her bloody tissue to her nose, heaved a dramatic, damsel-in-distress sigh and sank back down to the blacktop.

18
—
CLICK ON ONE OF THESE

"My turn to wipe the table!" Mickey took her dishes to the sink and grabbed a wet dishcloth.

"Thank you for doing your chores without being reminded." Ms. Lee brought her plate to the sink. "Your father and I appreciate that."

"We certainly do," Mr. Andrews said. He got a dry dish towel and followed behind Mickey, wiping up the water she dripped on the floor on her way from the sink to the table.

"Actually, it's her turn to take out the trash," Quinn said. "It's *my* turn to clear the table. She doesn't like doing the trash, so she's ..."

"I do *so* like the trash! And I do it the best." Mickey dropped the dishcloth on the table and marched back to the sink. "I could be a garbage man when I grow up. But I'd rather be a splinter doctor." Mickey took the trash out to the garage, giving herself a pep talk along the way. "There are lots of splinters in the world. A splinter doctor would never run out of patients."

Quinn wiped the table while his father dabbed water spots off the floor and his mother loaded the dishwasher. "May I do the rest of my computer time now?" Quinn asked. "I've got a little more than ten minutes left. I did some of it after school."

"That's fine," Mr. Andrews said. "It's already on; please don't close any open documents."

Quinn inserted the Fearless Froggie disk into the office computer. Although he'd been playing the game every day after school for two weeks, he was still at Level One—not one of his frogs had crossed the highway without getting squished. Quinn was determined to get to the next level, where your frog had to ford a river without getting chomped by an alligator, smacked by an angry beaver's tail, or speared by a heron's beak. Sam also had Fearless Froggie on his home computer, and claimed to have made it to Level Three, where frogs compete in a Fearless Froggie Olympics, complete with Froggie pole vaulting and Froggie bobsledding.

Mickey and her mother quietly entered the office. Mickey stood behind Quinn and their mother leaned against the doorjamb as Quinn deftly maneuvered his game's control pad and guided his frog across a busy five-lane, 95-miles-per-hour expressway. His frog dodged a motorcycle, an ambulance, a postal van, a

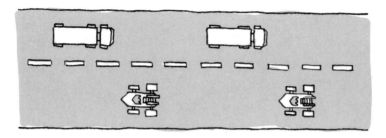

weaving furniture delivery truck, two speeding sports
cars full of shrieking teenagers, and three state trooper
cars in pursuit of the trucker and the reckless teens,
before it disappeared under the wheels of a elderly
man's Cadillac driving 25 miles per hour the wrong way
in the fast lane.

"Ah, foof!" Quinn sputtered.

"You're still not very good," Mickey said.

"Mickey," Ms. Lee said, "that's not nice."

"I know," Mickey sighed. "I just wanted to remind
him."

Ms. Lee rubbed her eyes. "Dessert, anyone? Nothing
fancy, just cereal and milk tonight."

"I didn't get to do my computer time today," Mickey
said.

"It's all yours." Quinn offered the chair to his sister.
"Have a squished frog for dessert." He followed his
mother back to the kitchen, where his father sat at the
table, pouring milk into his bowl of cornflakes.

"Can I have …"

"*May* I," Mr. Andrews corrected Quinn.

"May I have graham crackers and milk instead of cereal?"

"Of course." Quinn's mother removed a box of graham crackers from the cupboard, and leaned back against the kitchen counter. "My grandmother's favorite dessert was cereal," she said dreamily. "She said she'd rather have a bowl of cereal for dessert than a hot fudge sundae. I never saw her eat cereal for breakfast, not cold cereal. She'd have oatmeal on Sundays, before church. Other than that, it was two poached eggs over rye toast, every morning."

"Have we ever had any of those Yaweh's Disciples come to our house?"

Mr. Andrew paused, his spoon halfway to his mouth. "Interesting conversational transition," he said.

"Yes, we have, but it was some time ago." Ms. Lee brought the graham crackers and two more cereal bowls to the table and rested her hand on her husband's shoulder. "When was the last time you remember them stopping by here?"

"It's been two years, at least."

"How come we don't go to church?" Quinn pushed his graham crackers around his bowl with his spoon, mushing them into the milk. "Mom's grandma did. I'm just wondering."

Quinn carefully observed his parents. His dad grinned at his mom, who looked at his dad with the face she made when they played Scrabble and she accused him of making up words.

"Actually," Mr. Andrews said, "both your mom and I were raised in churchgoing families. Well, it was another generation back, in your mother's case. Grandpa and Grandma Lee are not churchgoers, as you know."

"Yes, my mother's parents went to church," Ms. Lee said. "To the church of *We're Right And Everyone Else Is Going to H-E-double—*"

"Your mother," Mr. Andrews interjected, "had a few negative experiences while visiting her grandparents' church, shall we say."

"Shall we say," Ms. Lee sniffed.

"But you did like the singing, as I recall." Mr. Andrews looked hopefully at his wife and winked at Quinn. "You know how she loves to sing."

"I don't need to sit in a building to sing. You can say amen to that." Quinn's mother had a spark in her eyes and a lilt to her voice. "I'm sorry, Quinn. I don't mean to be flippant."

"That's okay." Quinn tried not to smile. "You can be flippant all you like, 'cause I don't know what it means."

"It's one of those words Neally would look up, isn't it? I meant I'm not trying to ignore your question. My reasons ..."

"*Our* reasons," Mr. Andrews softly but firmly added.

"There are many reasons, some complicated, some clear-cut, why we don't go to a church, any church," Ms. Lee said. "Some of it is because we don't like the format, the way churches do things. We don't find it helpful, or interesting or meaningful. Some of it is because much of what is said and done by churches we simply don't think is true."

"Of course, there are other people who think differently," Mr. Andrews said. "They go to their church or temple, their mosque or meeting house, because they do find it meaningful."

"Or because somebody makes them go," Quinn said. "Like Tay. Even Sam and ..." Quinn's knee began to bounce under the table.

"Go on," Quinn's mother said. "We're listening."

"Lot of kids at my school go to lots of different churches. But when they talk about it, it's about how their parents made them go to Sunday school *and* youth league and so they had to miss soccer, or how they have to watch boring videos and do stupid crafts. David Greene missed his class's skate party because he has Hebrew school every weekend and can't miss even *one* Saturday."

"I think I'm coming up with some kind of disease."

Quinn and his parents turned to look at Mickey, who stood in front of the open refrigerator, looking deeply concerned. She held her hand over the light on the inside of the refrigerator door, and the skin between her thumb and forefinger glowed red.

"It drives me nuts when she creeps up like that," Ms. Lee whispered to her husband.

"Cereal or graham crackers?" Mr. Andrews asked Mickey.

Mickey did not answer, but joined her family at the table. "Peppy won't run on his wheel." Mickey stared pensively at her parents. "He might need hamster vitamins. When I grow up, I'll be a veterinarian for two hours a day, and a barber for the rest. And also have a museum."

"What happened to being a splinter doctor?" Quinn asked.

"Eh." Mickey flicked her hand as if to shoo a fly off her head. "May I have more computer time for dessert? My frog made it across all five lanes." She smiled at Quinn. "My sweet brother, you know how I feel when I'm good at something, darling? I get really rattley."

Quinn rolled his eyes.

"Mickey, you've still got plenty of computer time left," her father noted.

"I'll share my time, dear brother. What do you say, sweetie?"

"Ah, foof! I don't want to share it with you."

"Quinn, you always complain about Mickey teasing

you," Ms. Lee said. "Now she's being nice to you, and you're acting snotty to her."

"She's calling me 'darling.' That's not nice, Mom."

"Even if she is teasing, those are endearing terms. What's so bad about it?"

"I just don't like it," Quinn huffed. "It sounds like … like a *husband*."

"Oh my," Mr. Andrews said. "We can't have that."

"I'll share my Christmas candy." Mickey stuffed her hands into her pockets, withdrew her tightly clutched fists, and thrust her hands toward Quinn. "I have some mints left." Candy wrappers were visible between her clenched fingers. "Click on one of these."

"We're raising cyber geeks," Mr. Andrews sighed to his wife.

"No, thanks." Quinn stood up. "Okay, I'll share your computer time. Let's check on Peppy, first. Show me what you mean about him not playing on the wheel."

"My birthday's coming up." Mickey smiled up at Quinn as they walked down the hall towards the staircase. "Soon I'll be three days older than you."

"Actually, Mickey, I'm three *years* older than you," Quinn said.

"Three years?!" Mickey sounded impressed.

"I'll always be three years older than you. I was born three years before you were."

"Wow," Mickey said. "That was smart of you."

19
—

IT'S A GROWNUP THING

Quinn waved goodbye to his mother and climbed into
the backseat of Neally's car. He ran his fingers over the
worn leather of the driver's seatback. It felt cool and
smooth, like the skin of a lizard he'd caught in Sam's
backyard.

Last night on the telephone Quinn had eagerly
accepted Neally's offer of a ride, even as he wondered
aloud whether the thing in her driveway was truly a
car, and not a misplaced yard ornament. Neally didn't
mind Quinn's teasing; it was *she* who'd pointed out
the cobwebs in the car's wheel wells to Quinn. She'd
whispered into the phone that if her dad gave them a
ride to school, it would be one of the few times in her
life she'd seen him, or anyone, drive that car.

Quinn couldn't imagine why anyone would have a
car and not drive it. But Neally's family didn't seem to
have much use for a car. Neally walked to school, her

mother took the train to work, and her father rode his bicycle everywhere, even to the grocery store. But today was special: Mr. Standers had a load of supplies to take to school for their class's field trip.

"This is a cool car. It's so ..." Quinn searched for a better word than 'old.' "It's a classic."

"He means it's old. Yee-ow!" Neally feigned anger when Quinn shoved his book pack into her ribs. "Watch the seat belt!"

"I wasn't sure you'd be on time," Quinn said. "I didn't think the car would actually start."

"Me neither," Neally said.

"Me three-ther," said Mr. Standers. "I've only driven it twice since we moved here, but it started up like a charm. Right, Neally?"

Neally made hacking noises deep in her throat, as if she were a cat trying to bring up a hairball. "Sure thing, Dad. Just like a charm."

"It's a 1975." Mr. Standers stopped the car at the street corner and adjusted the rearview mirror. "These cars are built to last. Change the oil regularly and they'll run forever."

"Translation: we'll never get a new car in my lifetime," Neally muttered.

"How will the class be divided up when we get to the Noble Woods?" Quinn hoped to be in Mr. Standers' group, but didn't want to ask. Field trip assignments might be

one of those mysteries that adults weren't supposed to disclose to students.

"I'm not sure, Quinn. The last I spoke with your teacher she couldn't decide between choosing the groups alphabetically, having everyone count off one-two-three, or ..."

"If she still hasn't decided when we get there, don't say anything about which group you want to be in," Neally said. "If she thinks we want it a certain way, she'll do the opposite."

"Oh really?" Mr. Standers said.

"I wasn't talking to the front seat." Neally smiled innocently. "But yes, really." She looked at Quinn. "It's a grownup thing. They think it builds character, splitting us up and not letting us be with our same group of friends."

"Being with different people *is* how you make new friends," Mr. Standers said. "You get to see people in a new way when you're outside of your usual setting. You might appreciate people you never cared for or thought much about when you work together outdoors."

"Superb point, Dad. I can't wait to appreciate Brandon looking for a bathroom pass in the middle of the woods."

"All right." Mr. Standers cleared his throat. "No smart remarks from the peanut gallery."

"What's the peanut gallery?" Quinn asked.

"It's an elderly person's expression," Neally said. "The peanut gallery was in the back of a theatre, where the old geezers used to ..."

"Where dey put dem young whippersnappers!" Mr. Standers hunched over the steering wheel, as if he were one hundred years old. He smacked his gums and spoke in a high-pitched creak. "Dang young'uns make too much noise! Dad-gummit, who stole my teeth?"

The 1975 Volvo's peanut gallery wobbled with laughter.

"You can put me with the peanut gallery," Neally declared. "I don't care what group I'm in. I can work with anybody."

"Me too," Quinn quickly offered. "I don't mind being with kids I don't know, even if there's some I'd rather not be with."

"I read you," Neally said. "Matt Barker, ditto that."

"He's not my first choice." Quinn tried to sound detached, as if he were considering the respective merits of PB&J versus tuna sandwiches. "But it's no big deal."

"Matt is a classic example of what I was talking about. What's that flapping sound?" Mr. Standers pulled over to the side of the street. "The tarp is loose." He unfastened his seat belt, reached out the window, and tugged at the rope that secured a duffle bag to the car's roof. "Okay, where was I? If you got to see a different side of Matt, perhaps by working together to help restore a trail, or ..."

"Watch out," Neally whispered. "He's using his 'make-the-world-a-better-place' voice."

"... You might be surprised." Neally's father glanced over his shoulder and shifted the car into drive. "Matt could be a good friend to you, to anyone, if ..."

"If he were on another planet," Neally said.

"If he had a personality transplant," Quinn added.

"All right." The voice was stern, but Quinn saw that Mr. Standers was trying not to laugh.

"If he wasn't such a complete waste of chromosomes," Neally continued. "And a total disgrace to human DNA, and a gross example of ..."

"*No.*"

Quinn had never heard that simple syllable spoken with such quiet force. Mr. Standers stopped the car in the middle of the street without pulling over to the curb, and looked in the rear view mirror at his daughter.

"You do not talk about people that way, even if you think about them that way. *Never.* And if you find yourself thinking about someone that way, then you change the way you think."

Quinn held his breath, waiting for Neally to give her father evidence about Matt. She could tell what happened at the four square court, and Quinn could add so many other things. Neally stared into the mirror. She said nothing, but never broke eye contact with her father.

"Matt's a strong personality, no argument there. I gather he's been a bully over the years?"

Quinn looked at his shoes, at his seatbelt buckle, out the window, anywhere but in the rearview mirror. Mr. Standers had resumed driving and was speaking in his normal voice, but Quinn did not want Neally's father's caring, perceptive eyes focused on him.

"It's a shame, about Matt. In my experience, people give what they get in that regard."

Quinn didn't know what Mr. Standers meant, but he wasn't going to ask for an explanation. By the look on Neally's face, she wasn't going to, either. Quinn knew he shouldn't talk until Neally did. She'd been chewed out by her dad, and when your buddies get in trouble in front of you, you let them make the next move. You wait for them to act like everything is fine.

Mr. Standers turned onto the street that led to the school. "I've graded Matt's papers, worked with his reading group, and done some one-on-one with him. He's academically bright, if somewhat rigid. When I compliment his work he's surprised and grateful, though he pretends not to be." Mr. Standers sounded as if he were thinking out loud. "I don't think he often hears the kind of words he needs to hear."

"What kind of words?" Quinn's curiosity overcame his sense of buddy-honor.

"Simply that," Mr. Standers said. "Kind words."

"There's Lily's mom, Mrs. L'Sotho." Neally pointed to the school's main entrance, where a slender, tall African women stood. "I bet that's our line."

"I'll drop you off here," Mr. Standers said. "I'm meeting Ms. Blakeman in the faculty lot."

"Do you need help carrying the stuff?"

"No, but thanks for the offer, Quinn."

"I've seen my dad carry a tandem kayak all by himself, over his shoulder," Neally bragged to Quinn as they exited the car. They joined Sam and Tay and the other students standing in line by the curb. It looked as if their entire class was there.

"Why is *she* here?" Quinn glanced at Ms. Barnes, who was pacing in front of the *No Parking Bus Loading Zone Only* sign.

"She can tell we're waiting for a bus," Tay said.

"She can smell it," Sam added, "like how rabid wolves can smell fear."

"She's not our bus monitor," Quinn groused. "Can't she find some sixth graders to torture?"

As if she'd heard Quinn's suggestion, Ms. Barnes raised her whistle and turned her attention to the playground, where a group of older students loitered by the chain-link fence.

SSSSSSSQQQQQQQQQQQUUUUUUUURRRRRRK!

"Whose book pack is that by the gate?" Ms. Barnes strutted toward the fence.

"I love watching her hassle sixth graders," Sam said.

"I love watching her hassle anyone but me," Quinn said.

"Have you ever seen her from behind, when she's walking away from you?" Tay asked.

"I love it when she's walking away from me," Sam said.

"Look," Tay insisted. "She has the weirdest shape."

Quinn studied Ms. Barne's retreating form. "Yeah, weird. She's not exactly fat …"

"Groooooow-*tesque*!" Sam said gleefully. "Her head and shoulders and stomach are skinny, and then everything puffs out. I suspect there are mutant pear genes in her DNA."

"It's all that marching," Neally suggested. "Exercising a muscle makes it bigger."

Lily, who was in line in front of Neally, clapped her hand over her mouth. Arturo and Janos turned toward the sound of Lily's muffled giggles. *"Da!"* Janos joined in the laughter, shrugging his shoulders at Arturo, as if to ask what they were all laughing about.

"She's big." Arturo pretended to blow a whistle, and wiggled his hands by his hips. *"La Señora, nalgas grandes."*

Janos' eyes swelled as big as cow pies. *"Da, da!"*

· · · · · ·

"How inspirational!" Neally pinched her nostrils, sounding like the counselor who came to class once a month to drone on about how different cultures are good and different drugs are bad. "Unity in diversity! We're all multilingual when it comes to dissing our fearless leaders."

20

KA-WINN

Tay "knew" it would rain. Ha!

Quinn shaded his eyes against the vivid rays of sunlight that sliced through the canopy of towering Douglas fir trees. It was a good thing that the bus driver had known where to go. Now that his class was there, Quinn thought about how easy it was to miss the turnoff to the Noble Woods Nature Preserve. How many times had his family driven past the big grove of trees, forgetting that a forty-acre nature preserve was behind it?

Quinn wandered about the parking lot while the adults got organized. The bus ride had been uneventful, except for Brandon getting pelted by wads of paper and even someone's pair of mittens when he wondered aloud where a person might go to the bathroom if a person— not him, but any random person—had to go to the bathroom. Brandon noted in his defense that even in the woods, when you gotta go, you gotta go.

A laminated map of the Noble Woods was posted on a bulletin board at the north corner of the parking lot. Quinn checked out the map, which had faded and was covered with water spots. He returned to the bus, where Ms. Blakeman and Mr. Standers were dividing large plastic leaf bags, gardening tools, and work gloves into three piles.

Lily's mother began separating the students into three groups, calling out names from a list Ms. Blakeman had given her. Mrs. L'Sotho's voice was high and melodic, like Lily's. She had the darkest, most radiant skin Quinn had ever seen, like the surface of a deep, cool, and mysterious pond. Is it possible to see your reflection in someone else's skin? Quinn wondered.

Mrs. L'Sotho called out his name, pronouncing it in two syllables. "Ka-winn? Ka-winn Andrews-Lee?"

Quinn waved his hand. Mrs. L'Sotho waved back and pointed toward a group of students standing by the front of the bus. "Ka-winn, you will be with Mr. Standers' group. This group is complete. Now I will call the names for Ms. Blakeman's group, and you will please wait over there." Mrs. L'Sotho pointed toward a large oak tree by the park entrance trailhead.

"Ka-winn! Ka-winn!"

Quinn winced to hear Josh mimic Mrs. L'Sotho. He slumped toward the bus, thinking of something his father told him: be careful what you wish for because you might get it. Quinn had wanted to be in Mr.

Standers' group, but his heart dropped into his stomach when he saw that Josh and Matt were also in the group. He leveled his shoulders and tried to walk tall. What would Mickey do? *Look on the brighted side.*

There were three kids in his group that Quinn didn't know well: AnnaClaire, James, and Kristen. Quinn thought about what Neally's father had said: maybe, just maybe, he'd learn something interesting about them. All he knew so far was that they were three of the quietest kids in class. AnnaClaire always had her face in a book; James drew pictures of dinosaurs on all his papers, even spelling tests; Kristen hated to draw *anything*, and once had to stay after class when she'd refused to help color the elephant's tail for a wall mural their class had painted after their field trip to the zoo.

Looking on the *brighted* side, Arturo was in the group, and also Lily. Where was Janos? Who split up the Three Musketeers? Quinn spotted Janos in Mrs. L'Sotho's group. Janos looked like a lost puppy, slumped on the ground, holding his head in his hands, sitting between Neally and Tay, who were engaged in a spirited conversation. Quinn spotted Sam, who was in Ms. Blakeman's group, standing forlornly—yikes!—between Kelsey and Teena.

Click click, click click.

"Fifth graders! Welcome to the Noble Woods Preserve." Ms. Blakeman raised her hands overhead as if signaling a touchdown. "Your fearless leaders," she pointed to Mr. Standers and Mrs. L'Sotho, "have your project lists. We'll all start on the southwest trail. My group will go to the North Meadow; Mrs. L'Sotho's group will take the turnoff to Baker Rock; Mr. Standers' group will stop at the wetlands boardwalk and the Rock Creek bridge. All groups meet for lunch at North Meadow, eleven forty-five a.m. Fearless leaders, synchronize your watches." Ms. Blakeman checked her watch, and her glasses slid down her nose and clattered to the parking lot. "Whoa!" She retrieved her glasses and straightened the frame. "Maybe if I super-glued 'em to my earlobes ..."

Click click, click click.

"Everyone should have a trash bag and gloves. Your leaders have the tools for each group's task, which you'll begin as soon as you reach your destination. Fifth graders, ho!"

"Our 'destination'?" Quinn watched Mrs. L'Sotho's group follow Ms. Blakeman's.

"Sounds important, doesn't it?" said Mr. Standers.

"What's our group gonna do?" AnnaClaire asked.

"We'll be removing an invasive, non-native plant from the boardwalk," Mr. Standers explained. "That's the wooden part of the trail through a small wetlands area, by the bridge over Rock Creek. Also, we'll ... hey, Josh? Let's stay on the trail, so we don't trample the vegetation."

Josh tugged at a vine curling around the base of a massive Douglas fir tree that stood like a sentinel at the side of the southwest trail. "What's an evasive plant?" Josh asked.

"Road kill for brains," Matt muttered. "*In*-vasive. It's invading. And non-native means it's not from here, so it's not supposed to be here." He smiled at Mr. Standers. "Right?"

"That's essentially correct, Matt." Mr. Standers removed a field guide from his pocket. "Invasive, non-native species are those that are not natural to an area and are taking over habitat from the naturally occurring species."

"My mother's not a native," Kristen said solemnly. "She's from Minnesota."

"Dude!" Josh looked at Kristen as if she had an X carved on her forehead. "Sorry, but your mom's gotta go."

"Giant Reed Grass, here it is!" The students crowded around Mr. Standers, who showed them a picture in his field guide of a tall, brown-gray grass with fluffy plumes. "Funny you should mention Minnesota, Kristen. Some botanists believe the Giant Reed Grass was introduced here from the Midwest, specifically the Minnesota River Valley."

Kristen looked nervously around the group, as if she were about to apologize for something, Quinn thought. Then she saw the twinkle in Mr. Standers' eye, and her face relaxed.

"It's like feathers." AnnaClaire ran her slim fingers over the picture Mr. Standers pointed to.

"Yes," Mr. Standers said, "it's quite distinctive. Giant Reed Grass provides a good winter habitat for deer and rabbits. But it's invading the wetlands and meadows here, and crowding out the native ferns and grasses. Does everyone think they can recognize it?"

The students nodded enthusiastically and followed Mr. Standers up the southwest trail.

"Another assignment is to pick up trash along the way, and do a concentrated trash-sweep by the boardwalk and bridge. Remember, don't pick up anything unless you're wearing gloves, and even then, don't touch broken glass, sharp objects, or anything you can't identify."

"Like Josh's brain?" Matt piped up from the end of the group. "I don't think any of us could identify that from a road kill blob if we saw it, so watch your step."

Josh stuck out his tongue and slapped his palms to his head. "Anybody seen my brain? It looks like a squashed possum." Josh spoke as if his mouth was filled with soggy spaghetti.

The rest of the group joined in with Matt's laughter. Even Quinn had to admit that it was a funny remark. He forced himself to produce a few feeble chuckles as he worked his way to the front of the group and followed Mr. Standers into the woods.

21

VERY SMALL GUMWRAPPERS COULD BE HIDING

Mr. Standers divided his students into four working pairs: two pairs were assigned reed grass-pulling duties, and the other two pairs were to be the main trash patrol. Quinn was pleased to see that Mr. Standers had separated Matt and Josh. Quinn was partnered with Kristen, who acted as if their assignment, patrolling the left side of the trail, was vital to national security. She trailed behind Quinn, overturning twigs and leaves with the tip of her shoe and ignoring his occasional attempts at conversation. "Very small gum wrappers could be hiding" were the only words Quinn got out of her, even after he'd groused that she was checking the same spots he'd already gone over.

When they reached the boardwalk, Mr. Standers reminded the trash patrols to stay close to the sides and not trample the underbrush. He took the reed grass removers to the end of the boardwalk and helped them pull up the unwanted plants.

Quinn scrutinized the woods on either side of him. How little he'd noticed during his previous visits to the Noble Woods, when he'd tramped over the boardwalk as if it were just another part of the trail. Now he saw that it was a carefully constructed section of wooden two-by-fours spanning a grassy area that, Mr. Standers said, was often flooded during the early winter months. Someone had gone to a lot of trouble to build it, Quinn thought. He began to search the surrounding grasses and underbrush with renewed spirit, silently rejoicing when he found a stash of mud-encrusted bottle caps at the base of a large sword fern.

Quinn took a break, and set his bag atop a mossy stump. Matt and his partner AnnaClaire, and Josh and Lily pulled up tufts of reed grass that poked up between the planks of the boardwalk. Mr. Standers was clearing a large patch of reed grass to the right of the boardwalk. Arturo and James were on trash patrol behind Mr. Standers. Quinn noted with a mixture of pride and disgust the size of the trash bags the boys dragged behind them. It was satisfying to see how much they'd done, but how did all the junk get here in the first place? he wondered. Fast food wrappers, crumpled cigarette packs—what kind of people dump trash in the woods?

Quinn looked up at the sky, no longer needing to shield his eyes against the sun. Billowy white and gray clouds were invading the rapidly shrinking patches of blue. Invading; no, that was the wrong term. Clouds might be invasive, but they were definitely a native species in Oregon. Quinn wished Sam and Neally, even Tay, were with him to hear and appreciate his clever thought. The air had that musty, it's-gonna-rain smell. Perhaps Tay's prediction was on track. What was it Neally had said last week, when Sam asked her how she felt about living in Hillsboro? *If you don't like the weather, don't worry. It'll change in five minutes.*

Quinn held his breath for a moment, and found the lack of noise unsettling. He slowly exhaled, closed his eyes, and realized that it wasn't so silent after all.

The absence of human chatter was what had caught his attention. If he listened closely he could detect the distant, rapid *tap-tap-tap* of a woodpecker, the twitterings of squirrels, and the calls of songbirds. But except for the rustle of plastic sacks there was almost no sound from Quinn's fellow humans.

Mr. Standers' group worked in diligent silence. They were friendly and focused; Quinn even caught Matt giving Lily an admiring glance when she helped Josh pull up a stubborn shaft of reed grass that had wrapped itself around a slender aspen. The pairs worked side by side, separately and yet together. Quinn began to appreciate the idea of teamwork, a word he'd always thought had to do with sports, and he thought again about what Mr. Standers had said.

Quinn stepped off the boardwalk into damp grasses to retrieve an aluminum can that gleamed from beneath a bush. He inhaled deeply through his nose, trying to identify the aromas that surrounded him. Some scents were predictable: wet earth, moss-covered wood, and stagnant water. Others seemed familiar but out of place. What was it—a plant? An animal?—that smelled like the minty ointment Quinn's father used when he pulled a muscle in his back?

Mr. Standers strode to the middle of the boardwalk. He checked his watch, placed his hands on his hips, pursed his lips, and let out a low whistle. "Magnificent! And I'm not only talking about the scenery. Before we move on to the bridge, take a good look at what you've done."

The students beamed with satisfaction. Not one scrap of paper littered the grasses or bushes, and the boardwalk and the surrounding grounds were free of the feathery reed grass.

Kristen held up a piece of faded orange paper the size of a pinkie-finger Band-Aid. She dropped it into her sack, which appeared to be empty except for that one piece of debris. "Yes!" she hissed triumphantly. "Is it time for lunch yet?"

22

THE THREE TRASHKETEERS

"The skies are beautiful in Hillsboro; they change so often! Do you native Oregonians appreciate that?" Neally let herself fall back onto the thick green grass in the North Meadow. She rolled over onto her stomach, reached for her lunch sack, and grinned at Quinn and Sam. "If you grew up here you might take it for granted."

After everyone met up at the North Meadow, Ms. Blakeman announced that the groups could temporarily disband for lunch. Although they'd need to rejoin their groups for the return to the bus, the students could eat lunch with whomever they chose. Quinn, Neally, and Sam used their parkas to improvise a picnic blanket on the grass under an oak tree in the middle of the meadow. Quinn checked his lunch bag. The short, squatty thermos meant his mom had packed his favorite lunch: leftover pasta.

"Macaroni and cheese for Master Andrews-Lee!"

Sam sang out. He frowned at his own baloney sandwich, which had gotten squashed by his apple. "Welcome to our destination, sanitized for your protection by those Master Trash Collectors, Ms. Blakeman's Rakemen."

"You worked here, in the North Meadow?" Neally gave Sam an admiring grin. "Nice job."

"You wouldn't believe how much trash there was before your groups got here," Sam said.

"Oh, yes, I would," Quinn replied.

"I was a Master Trash Locator," Sam said.

"Me too," Neally said.

"Me three!" Quinn added.

"The Three Trashketeers!" Neally raised her hand and exchanged high-fives with the boys. "Hey, Lily!" Neally jumped to her feet and waved to Lily, who stood by her mother at the far end of the meadow. "Do you think Lily will want to eat with us?"

"Too late." Sam pointed to Arturo and Janos, who had joined Lily's mother.

"She was a weed-puller in our group," Quinn said.

"We Trashketeers must stick together," Sam said. "We are noble, but underappreciated. No sharing our hard-earned meal break with weed-pullers."

"Oh, spare me," Neally groaned. "We didn't have any weed-pullers, just Trash Masters and Trail Clearers. I don't think the Trail Clearers worked as hard as us Trash Masters."

"Ditto that," Sam said.

"I chose Janos for a partner, which was a superb choice if I do say so myself. And I just did." Neally took a swig from her water bottle. "He has Superman X-ray vision when it comes to spotting candy wrappers. I bet we picked up twice as much as Tay and Brandon."

"We work together; the many are one." Sam spoke in his robot voice. "This is not a competition, Ms. Standwell."

"I know that. But we see who works hard and who doesn't, no matter what the adults say."

"How come your group got to choose partners?" Quinn asked.

"We didn't," Neally said. "When Ms. Blakeman said she'd randomly assign partners—like we'd believe *anything* assigned is random—a few kids made faces. I could tell someone was going to say something mean if they were paired with Janos, so I asked to be his partner."

"Matt ... *HEE-ACK!*" Quinn choked on a mouthful of macaroni. He shook his head and waved away Sam, who had raised his hand above Quinn's shoulder blades as if he were going to slap him on the back. "I'm okay," Quinn gasped. He took a sip of water.

"Mac-ahack-aroni? An honorable Trashketeer must not talk about food and eat food at the same time," Sam said.

"He wasn't talking about food." The jungle-cat look crept into Neally's eyes, which had darkened to the color of the meadow grass. "He was going to say something about Matt." She rolled over onto her back and shaded her eyes with her hand.

Even though they were in the middle of the meadow, at least thirty feet away from anyone else, Quinn lowered his voice. "Your dad put Lily and Matt together. But Matt didn't want to be with her, so he put Lily and Josh together."

"What—no way!" Neally abruptly sat up stiff and tall. "My dad would never let anyone say a mean thing about ..."

"Would you let me finish?" Quinn snapped.

Neally's mouth opened and closed without making a sound. She looked at Quinn as if she'd forgotten who he was, and seemed both embarrassed and impressed.

"Your dad didn't let anyone do anything, okay?"

"Righty-o." Sam's eyes blinked rapidly. He'd never heard that strong of a tone come from Quinn. He picked pieces from his sandwich and tossed them to a blackbird that hopped around the base of the oak tree. "How did Neally's dad know Matt didn't want to be with Lily?"

"When your dad started naming the partners, Matt was right next to him. Your dad called out me and Kristen for trash, then Matt and Lily. But he didn't get 'Lily' out; it was like, 'Matt and Li—' and Matt got this weird look. His eyes got all big, and he jerked his chin, like he was nodding 'No' to Mr. Standers but didn't want the rest of us to see it." Quinn looked around the meadow. "Lily was putting her gloves on. She didn't notice; I don't think anyone else did."

"You did," Sam said.

"And your dad." Quinn nodded at Neally, who still looked defensive. "He just went right on. He said, 'Matt and Lily will be reed pullers, teamed with AnnaClaire and Josh.' Real smooth, like it was his first choice."

"Can anyone join this crew, or is it invitation only?" Neally's father shaded his eyes as he walked toward the oak tree. "Make up your mind," Mr. Standers pleaded to the sky in mock exasperation. "Will we be tanning or dripping?"

"Tanning?" Sam rolled up his sleeve and tapped his fingers against the freckles on his pale skin. "Does not compute."

Quinn held his arm out and compared it with his friend's. "I'm way darker than you."

"Way?" Sam smirked. "Lily is way. You are barely way."

"Hi, Dad. We just finished eating." Neally stood up and pulled her parka out from underneath Quinn's thermos, and Quinn looked longingly at the rest of his lunch. "We're going to check out a stream over there," Neally said, pointing to the southeast corner of the meadow, "before we have to head back."

Quinn and Sam exchanged what-is-she-talking-about? glances. "That's exactly what we're going to do," Quinn said. Neally stuck out her tongue at Quinn, but her eyes were merry.

"Care for some company?" Mr. Standers looked at his watch. "We've got a few minutes before the clicker tolls."

"Most certainly." Sam grabbed his pack and tied his parka around his waist.

The three students and one adult headed for the stream. Sam rolled his sleeves back down, and Mr. Standers pointed at Sam's forearm. "I had an aunt who said freckles came from angel kisses." Sam's face reddened, and Mr. Standers quickly added, "But she was a crazy old bat."

Neally ran up the footbridge that crossed over the small stream. "This is more like a pond," she said, leaning over the handrail. "The water's barely moving. I can see my reflection."

Sam tossed a pebble over the handrail. Quinn looked into the water. "It's like her skin." He felt three pairs of eyes upon him, and realized he'd spoken his thought aloud. "Lily's mom," he explained. "She's got the sparkliest skin." He rolled up his sleeve and rested his forearm on the handrail. One by one Neally, Sam, and Mr. Standers did the same.

"Cool!" Neally said. "You move down there." She directed her father to trade places with Quinn so that the four arms were lined up in order of increasing brownness, from Sam to Quinn to Neally to her father. "We could do the whole class. Kelsey would be there," she pointed at the spot in front of Sam.

"And Arturo there," Quinn said as he pointed to the spot between Neally and her father, "and Teena ..." He closed his eyes and tried to picture his classmates.

"And Brandon there!" Sam pointed toward a port-o-potty at the far corner of the meadow. He looked thoughtfully at Mr. Standers. "Why is Lily's skin so much lighter than her mom's?"

Quinn felt uneasy, but wasn't sure why. He had wondered the same thing himself. For all the talk of how wonderful people were because of their differences, it seemed to Quinn that adults often pretended not to notice the differences, and then acted annoyed or embarrassed when the kids did. But Mr. Standers wasn't the least bit troubled by Sam's question.

"Lily's family is multi-ethnic. That means ..."

"We didn't just fall off the diversity truck," Neally huffed. "We know what that means."

"Daughter, must I invoke the dreaded Peanut Gallery Rule?"

Quinn and Neally giggled. Sam looked confused. Mr. Standers spoke to Sam, using an accent Quinn had heard in an old vampire movie. "Ve shall ignore des peasants." He nodded at Neally and Quinn. He continued in his regular voice. "Lily's mom is from Namibia, in Africa. Lily's dad was born in the United States, and his parents were from Northern Africa and France."

"That's way more interesting than being from Spokane," Neally sighed.

"Think of the frequent flyer miles they could earn, going to family reunions," Sam noted.

"I've never been to another country," Quinn said, "but I was named after my Dad's friend, who lives in Ireland."

Click click, click click.

Ms. Blakeman stood in the center of the meadow. She turned slowly in a circle with her hands held above her head, her frog clicker inside a piece of paper that she had folded into a cone shape, like a megaphone.

"That's our five minute warning. Remember where we regroup?" Mr. Standers looked around the meadow, his gaze stopping at the oak tree. "Whose bottles are those?"

Neally and Sam scampered to fetch their water bottles. Mr. Standers leaned back against the handrail. "You look ready to go," he said to Quinn. Quinn nodded, picked up a handful of pebbles, and dropped them one by one into the water.

"So tell me, Quinn, what do you like to do?"

Quinn froze for a moment, but just a moment. "I like dropping rocks into water."

Mr. Standers sounds like Neally when he laughs. Quinn was pleased to have sparked that laugh from Mr. Standers. Everything Quinn knew about Neally's father made Quinn think that Mr. Standers didn't expect the usual answers to the usual questions. Quinn hated it when adults asked him the what-do-you-do question because he knew what they really were after. They wanted you to talk about what distinguished you from other kids. They wanted you to spew your list of hobbies, your many accomplishments in sports, your baseball or game card collections—things kids get known for.

Mickey could at least talk about her swimming. Quinn was looking for something to call his own; something to make him special. He had confided that to Neally, on the way home from school, just last week.

Your name goes on the certificate if your class wins the community service project, he'd said. Your own, individual name, not just your class. And the names are carved into a plaque, which goes up at city hall, and stays there forever, for everyone to see.

Quinn wondered if Neally had said anything to her father. *No, she wouldn't do that.* Quinn handed some pebbles to Mr. Standers, and they stood in comfortable silence for a minute, dropping the small rocks over the handrail into the water.

"Time to join up," Mr. Standers said. He and Quinn headed for the drinking fountain at the southwest corner of the meadow, where the rest of their group gathered around their equipment. Mr. Standers began counting tools and gloves.

"The rest of the groups have already left." James glanced anxiously toward the trail.

"We can catch up," Mr. Standers said. "I just want to make sure we've got everything."

"Aren't we done?" Josh asked.

"We'll double check for trash on the way back, but yes, we're finished." Mr. Standers looked around the meadow. "We're missing seven gloves. Three of the smaller pairs, and one of the larger ones. Who used the smaller pairs?"

Lily smiled shyly. "It was mine, the big one. I ate there, with my mother." She pointed toward a grassy knoll on the other side of the stream.

"Lily, James, AnnaClaire, and Arturo, you come with me and we'll check for the gloves," Mr. Standers said. "The rest of you take the trash bags and go on ahead. If we haven't caught up by the bridge you can keep going, but wait for us at the boardwalk."

Matt, Josh, Quinn, and Kristen started back on the trail. As soon as they were out of sight of the North Meadow, Matt and Josh ran ahead, leaving Quinn and Kristen behind. Kristen clutched her trash bag in one hand, and leaned down to pick a purple wildflower from the right side of the trail. She put the flower behind her right ear and looked around for another one. Quinn walked down the trail, thinking he should remind Kristen that she shouldn't pick wildflowers. Hadn't she heard Ms. Blakeman's instructions? It was against city regulations.

"Hey, Kristen?" Quinn turned around. Kristen gave no indication that she'd heard him. She was twenty feet behind him, on her hands and knees, intently examining the left side of the trail. "Something yellow," she mumbled.

Fine, Quinn said to himself. Let Mr. Standers catch up and play nature cop. He continued alone down the trail, noting with approval that there was not one bit of trash anywhere he looked.

23
—

BRANDON
KNOWS HOW
TO SPELL

No—no no no! Why did it have to be me!?

Quinn dropped his trash bag. Matt and Josh were
sitting on the railings on the bridge over Rock Creek.
They doubled over with laughter as they looked down at
the chalk-streaked planks of the bridge.

Ducks Rule! Beavers Drol!

Quinn stood as if he'd sprouted roots. Matt and Josh
hadn't spotted him yet. The slogans were also scrawled
on the railings and side supports, in huge, bright pink
and blue chalky letters, and in each case the word
"drool" was misspelled "drol."

Josh hopped off the railing and wiped his hands on
his pants, leaving a pink streak down the side of his
jeans. "No, wait," Matt said. He whacked his gloves
against Josh's legs, dusting off the telltale chalk, then
wiped the dust off his gloves on the grass by the side

of the bridge. Quinn saw a pink splotch on the seat of Matt's jeans, just the kind of mark a large piece of painter's chalk might leave if you pulled it out of your pocket.

"Uh oh."

Quinn started at the sound of Kristen's voice. Matt and Josh whirled around, and Matt's eyes narrowed into slits.

"How long have they been ..."

"Shut up," Matt shushed Josh.

Kristen stood three feet behind Quinn, fingering the purple, yellow, and white flowers she'd tucked behind her ear. Matt looked right through Kristen; Quinn turned around and saw the rest of their group approaching the bridge.

"Hey, Mr. Standers." Matt waved his arm. "Look what happened—somebody messed up our clean bridge!"

Mr. Standers dropped his duffle bag. He hugged his arms across his chest and shook his head. "Does anyone know ..."

"It was already here. It must have been one of the other groups. They went first." Josh ignored the *shut up, dummy* glare Matt gave him. "It was already here when we got here."

"Well, we're not leaving until it's *not* here." Mr. Standers reached into his duffle bag. "Everyone put their gloves on and dip them in the water, right here, by the creek bank. We'll scrub it down."

Arturo, AnnaClaire, and Quinn already had their gloves on, and one by one they dipped them into the pond. Mr. Standers tossed gloves to the other students and dipped his own into the water. He looked at Kristen, Quinn, Matt, and Josh. "I'll ask again, did anyone see anything?"

"I saw *them*." Kristen pointed at the three boys.

"I bet it was Brandon." Matt's voice was as cool as lemonade, and he looked calmly at Mr. Standers. "Mrs. L'Sotho's group was ahead of ours."

"Yeah, Brandon always brings chalk to school, and he's always saying, 'Go Ducks.'" Josh's nervous laughter sounded as if he were attempting to choke a chicken with his tongue.

"But Brandon's parents went to Oregon State, not U of O," AnnaClaire said thoughtfully. "Brandon's a Beavers fan," she explained to a puzzled Mr. Standers.

"And Brandon knows how to spell." Quinn concentrated on relaxing his fists as all eyes turned to him.

Mr. Standers raised his hand, and the students in his group knew that they were not to speak unless spoken to. He focused his steady gaze upon Quinn. His curious but firm expression let everyone know he suspected that Quinn had seen something.

"Go on," Mr. Standers said gently.

Quinn could feel Matt and Josh staring at him, as if their eyes were hurling javelins between his shoulder blades. He told himself everything would be fine as long as he didn't look at them. He fixed his eyes on Mr. Standers' beard and described what he'd seen.

"What a liar!" Matt said scornfully, even as he desperately craned his head to look at the seat of his pants. Mr. Standers grabbed Matt's hand before Matt could wipe off the chalk. Mr. Standers looked at Matt's pants, then at the words on the bridge. "Josh, come here." Mr. Standers crouched low, ran his fingers down the side of Josh's pant leg, and held up his chalky finger. Josh shifted from foot to foot, as if he were Brandon after drinking a six-pack of soda.

Arturo crawled out onto the bridge on his hands and knees and wiped at the graffiti with his gloves. "*Problemas*," he muttered. "*Problemas grandes*."

AnnaClaire tried to sound cheerful. "If we all help it'll only take a few minutes."

"Thank you, Arturo and AnnaClaire. Everyone get to work." Mr. Standers spoke slowly, with a quiet, dreadful firmness in his tone that had the students wishing he were yelling instead. He turned to Matt and Josh. "Not one word to each other, do you understand? Josh, you're in the back of the line. Matt, up front with me. I'll talk with each of you, separately, when we get to the parking lot."

24

I HAVE MANY SECRETS

"Fifth graders, it seems we've ... fifth graders? FIFTH GRADERS?!"

Click click, click click.

The driver scowled as the clicker, amplified by Ms. Blakeman's makeshift paper megaphone, ricocheted through the bus. Ms. Blakeman stood at the front of the bus and announced that despite having to wait an extra twenty minutes for Mr. Standers' group to catch up, they'd made it back in time for the tail end of lunch recess.

"Please take your packs with you. Mrs. L'Sotho, Mr. Standers, and I will take care of the equipment. And before we leave please take a moment to think about ..." Ms. Blakeman's glasses fogged up. She lowered her chin, let them slide down her nose, and wiped the lenses clean with a bandanna she wore around her neck. "What a magnificent job you did! I hope you all appreciate that."

She dabbed her eyes with the bandanna. "You've fifteen minutes left of recess, so make the most of it. And what do we say to our fearless leaders?!"

YEEEEEEEEEEEEEEEEEEEEEEEEEEAH!

It sounded as if a busload of Kelsey Kings burst into cheers, and the driver covered his ears. Ms. Blakeman's class stampeded out of the bus and headed for the playground, all but Matt and Josh, who followed Mr. Standers and Ms. Blakeman into the school's administrative office.

Quinn ignored the sound of his name being called and jogged toward the field. It hadn't rained for a couple of days; no whistle was going to keep him from running today.

"Hey, Quinn." Neally walked as fast as she could, looking right and left for the playground supervisor. She broke into a run a few feet before she reached the field. Neally pumped her arms up and down, her pace smooth and confident, but Quinn had a head start. "Wait up! Are you training for a marathon?"

Quinn ran even faster. It seemed to help untangle the knot in his stomach.

"Could you please wait up?"

Quinn slowed his pace to a jog, then to a fast walk.

"You're not even breathing hard," Neally panted. "You're in better shape than I thought."

Quinn raised one eyebrow in an attempt to look mysterious. "I have many secrets."

"Not as many as you think. I sat next to AnnaClaire on the bus. Boy, that girl can talk when she's got a story to tell. And Tay was right behind us, listening in. He's such a snoop. Look at him now, playing secret agent."

Quinn's eyes followed Neally's finger, which pointed toward the administrative building. Tay had pressed himself against the wall, by the window next to the building's back door. He alternately peeked through the window and flattened himself back against the wall, then suddenly pushed himself away from the wall and ran toward Neally and Quinn. The door flung open and Matt, followed by Josh, exited the administrative building.

"Nice going," Tay huffed to Quinn.

"You're welcome," Quinn replied.

"What did you find out?"

"Josh caved to your dad," Tay answered Neally. "A total admission. He's such a wimp. And it isn't even such a big deal. The chalk came off, most of it."

"Do they get detention?" Quinn asked hopefully.

"Nah. They don't even have to miss recess, just stay after school for a writing assignment."

"'We will not do stupid things. We will not *be* stupid things ...'" Neally feigned scribbling on a sheet of paper.

"But get this, Ms. Blakeman called their parents! Matt's dad is going to go into orbit." Tay looked gravely at Quinn. "You better watch your back."

"Why'd it have to be me?" Quinn beseeched the sky. "I *had* to be the one that saw them."

"But you didn't have to be the one to tell."

"What *are* you?" Neally looked at Tay as if he'd asked Quinn to stomp on a newborn baby chick. "What kind of a person are you?"

A familiar voice rumbled behind Neally. "He's a loser kind of person, if he hangs out with this rat."

Tay laughed uneasily and jammed his hands into his pockets. Neally turned to face Matt. She ignored Josh, who as usual was two steps behind Matt. "So brave of you to tiptoe up on us," she said icily.

Quinn's heart rose when he saw Neally's composure. He'd made a choice at the Noble Woods to tell the truth, now he had to choose to respond to the next thing Matt would do. With Matt, there was always a next thing.

"Chalk on a bridge, oh, disaster! Go run and tell Neally's daddy!" Matt sneered at Quinn. "Everyone hates a rat."

"A rat *fink*," added Josh.

"Yes, everyone hates finks," Neally said. "Especially finks who try to pin the blame on someone else for what *they* did. Did you think anyone would believe Brandon would do something so lame?"

Quinn stretched his shoulders and filled his lungs with cool air. "Besides, Brandon's the best speller in class."

"The best speller, wow, that makes sense," Josh snickered.

"Everyone knows he is, Josh," Neally said.

"And everyone knows you can't even spell your own name." Quinn folded his arms across his chest. "You misspelled 'drool.'"

"It has *two* o's," Neally said. "Like nincompoop."

Josh's face turned purple and his lower lip wobbled.

"It's over, all right, okay?" Tay pleaded to Matt. "Big whoopee. Let's play tag, or something else before recess is totally wasted, okay?" Tay's voice rose to a squeak on the *okays*.

Neally looked at Tay as if he were an oozing scab. A light switched on behind her eyes, and she turned to Matt. "Good idea," she said. "Let's play tag. I declare a challenge."

Quinn knew Neally was up to something. The first one who declared a challenge got to pick the two tag leaders, who in turn got to pick their team members.

"I'm Captain One; Tay, you're Captain Two. I pick Matt and Quinn, and we'll get Kelsey, and ..." Neally looked around the school yard. "Where's Lily? She's fast, once she gets going."

"Josh, you're with me," Tay said. "I get Sam and Arturo, they're over at four square, and James and ..."

Neally cupped her hands around her mouth and yelled across the schoolyard. "Hey, Lily!" She turned to Matt and smiled sweetly. "You don't mind having Lily on our team?"

"Why should I care?" Matt stared vacantly at Neally.

"Who cares who's on anyone's team?" Tay groused. "I'm rounding up mine. Be on the field in one minute or you gotta forfeit one player." Josh followed Tay toward the blacktop.

"If you don't care who's on the team then why wouldn't you be partners with Lily at the Noble Woods?"

What are you doing!? Quinn desperately tried to transmit a silent but urgent message into the space between Neally's ears. *The Mighty Quinn says ZIP IT, Neally.*

Matt glared at Quinn.

"Why are you looking at Quinn? My father is the one who told me you wouldn't work with Lily," Neally lied. "What's your problem?"

"I don't have a problem. I like to choose, that's all."

"So, you chose AnnaClaire?"

"No, I didn't choose AnnaClaire. Your dad did."

"I still don't understand." Neally hesitated, as if confused. "You say you like to choose, so why didn't you mind when you got another partner if you also didn't get to choose that partner?"

Matt cocked his head. He looks more intrigued than angry, Quinn thought. He's been challenged, and he knows it.

"Groups don't matter in class or sports. People can mix if they want. But when it's one-on-one ..." Matt

tugged at his ear. "It's
natural, to want to be
separate, with your own
kind."

"Your own *kind*?"
Neally quickly
transformed her snort
into a cough. "That's
interesting, Matt.
Who told you that?"

"No one had to
tell me, it's obvious.
It's what God wants."

Neally waved to Lily, who was approaching the field.
"I'm not sure I understand. Your god wants us to be
separate, but here we all are, together. Un-separate."

"People are different because God made them that
way. He wants us to be different. It says so in his word,
his rules, he wants ..."

"*His* word? *His* rules? So, your god's a guy? You
know, a man, a dude?"

"Well ... he's male ... yeah." Matt looked puzzled.

"Oh. So, tell me," Neally asked, in mock, wide-eyed
sincerity, "does he shave?"

Quinn reached down and pretended to tie his
shoelace. He knew if he made eye contact with Neally, it
was all over.

"God could shave if he wanted to." Matt shrugged his shoulders. "He can do anything he wants, but that's not the point. He wants us to do what *he* wants."

Matt's eyes glazed over, and seemed to focus on a spot far across the schoolyard. His voice was vague and vacant, as if he were trying to recall a long-forgotten speech.

"It's important to be different, and stay different, like he made us. If we're all the same, then we're not different, and that's why we need to keep with our same kind, 'cause if we don't, eventually we'll end up ... like, a gray mess. It's all there, in God's word. My dad knows, and you could too." Matt looked earnestly at Neally and Quinn. "You could understand, if you read God's word. If you read it *right*. Someone can help you go to church and understand about it."

"Hey, I'll try anything," Neally said. "Wait a sec, both of Lily's parents are pastors. I'll ask her if I can visit their church. I could get two helps at once."

"That's not a good idea." Matt bit his lip. "You can't just go anywhere—if something's important, you have to do it right. You have to find the right place to learn."

"I get it." The innocence faded from Neally's voice. "'Right' for you means what someone else thinks *you* should think." Neally yawned. "*I* think I'll pass on that."

"But doesn't being different mean having different ideas?" Quinn thought of something his mother had said, and for the first time in his life he felt sorry for Matt. "If you say that there's a god but it's only in one place and not another, that's like saying it's locked in a special box ..."

"Or in a book," Neally added.

"That only some people can open," Quinn finished.

"No, you're wrong, both of you!" Matt's voice shook. "You're so wrong. He *is* in everything, but not everyone—I mean, you gotta look in the right everything."

"Everywhere."

"Everywhere?" Neally turned around, toward the sound of Lily's melodic voice. "Then I could look on the field?"

Lily smiled bashfully, her hand fluttering around the neck of her bright red, orange, and yellow striped dress. "There is a song we would sing." She kicked at a pebble, pointed to the ground, then to the schoolyard and up to the clouds. "It for was this." She circled her arm over her head. "All of this."

"But there's more!" Matt slapped his fist against his leg and shifted from side to side. "It's not just pretty nature stuff and—you can't just say it's ... argh!" He stomped his foot as the end-of-recess buzzer rang out.

Saved by the bell, Quinn gloated.

Neally grinned and said, "Somebody sing 'Amen.'"

25

THE LAW OF
PROPORTIONALITY

"Shouldn't we wait for Sam?" Neally glanced back toward the school.

"His sister's picking him up. He's got a piano recital, then Scouts. C'mon." Quinn quickened his pace, his sneakers slapping the sidewalk. "Matt's gonna hate me for infinity."

"I don't think Matt is allowed to believe in infinity."

"Ha ha. Really, this is serious, Neally. If Matt gets in trouble with his dad, he'll make my life miserable."

"I thought he already did that."

"Fine, even more miserable. Mega, giga-miserable."

"Don't worry." Neally picked up a stick and ran it across a fence they walked past. She spoke in time with the stick's *tap-tap* against the fence posts. "You-will-rise-to-the-oc-ca-sion."

"Yeah, right." Quinn tried to snatch the stick from Neally, who laughed and tossed it over the fence.

"Besides, in the next couple of years if Matt doesn't

grow any taller or nicer, some meaner and bigger boy will kick his butt in middle school. It's called the law of proportionality. Something my dad told me."

A slow smile warmed Quinn's face. "That is a most excellent law."

"Can you stop at my house? You have to see this: Yin and Yang got a hold of some newspapers from our recycling bin. They built a nest in the living room and they sit in it, like a pair of hawks. My mother says they're having an identity crisis."

"Sure—ah, foof, I can't. I told Mickey I'd help her with her mouse."

"You got a new pet and didn't tell me?"

"It's not a pet, it's dead. Mickey found it, and she wants to give it a funeral."

"That's considerate of her. But you could still stop and see the nest. Oh, I almost forgot!" Neally flapped her arms in excitement. "My dad wants to ask you if ..."

"Quinny Quinny Quinny, Neally Neally Neally!"

Neally whirled around and looked at the small figure that was rapidly catching up with them. "Who is *that*?"

"Guess I forgot to tell you about Mickey's new haircut."

"I believe the proper term is clear cut," Neally said dryly. "Haircuts usually leave some hair on the head."

Mickey doubled over when she reached Quinn and Neally. She put her hands on her knees and took deep, exaggerated breaths.

"Hey, Mickey, what's with your new do?"

Mickey beamed at Neally. "I got it yesterday. Mom took me to the snippin' shop after dinner." Mickey lowered her head. "Go on, pet it. I know you want to."

Neally ran her fingers over the short stubble. What was left of Mickey's hair was both soft and bristly, and streaked with red, blue, green, and gold hair paint. "Mickey, this is unbelievably cool! You look like a tropical macaw."

"Thanks. But the teacher called my mom after recess and told her I can't use hair paint anymore. It's too distincting to the rest of the class."

"You mean, *distracting*," Quinn said.

"That too," Mickey said. "It'll be great for swimming. And I can run even faster, without all that hair to catch up in gravity."

"Let's get going," Neally said. "Quinn said he's going to help with your mouse funeral."

"He's brother of the year! But I've changed my mind. No funeral." Mickey spun in a circle, holding tight to the straps of her book pack. "Do you ever wonder, how does the world work?" She staggered, struggling to get her balance. "How does the world spin without air?"

"I don't know what you mean," Quinn said. "Try asking it a different way."

"I don't think so," Mickey said. "That could get confusing."

"Hey, parrot-head." Neally placed her hand on

Mickey's shoulder. "Would you like to see my cats' idea of a bird's nest?"

"Yes and yes again!" Mickey hugged Neally. She pulled away from the hug and pointed behind Neally. "Could Tay come too?"

"Why are they walking this way?" Neally griped. "Matt lives on the other side of school."

"There's a Scout meeting at Tay's house," Quinn whispered as the boys approached.

"Hey, cancer *cabeza*!" Tay ran his hand over Mickey's colorful head. "Lookin' cool."

Mickey had always liked Tay and was obviously pleased with his attention. She giggled and batted at Tay's hand. Quinn winced, then told himself that Tay wasn't teasing her in a mean way, even if the cancer remark was strange.

"Cancer *cabeza*?" Neally said suspiciously.

"*Cabeza* means head in Spanish," Tay said.

"Ask Arturo, if you don't believe him," Matt added.

"Mickey kinda looks like my Aunt Jenny," Tay continued. "She got cancer, and her medicine made her hair fall out, so one day she just shaved her head."

"My, what a pleasant association." Neally used her puffed-up, Queen of England voice.

"I bet you'll cut a few seconds off your swim time," Tay said to Mickey.

"Or you could just wear a boy's swimsuit," Matt said.

"No, I can't," Mickey objected. "I'm a girl."

"A girl parrot," Quinn said solemnly.

"Oh, so you're a girl?" Matt persisted. "Then how come you cut your hair like a boy?"

"I'm not wearing hair like a boy. I'm a girl, so it's a girl haircut."

"Girls' hair is supposed to be long. Guys have short hair."

"Hair is hair, Matt," Neally said. "If you let it grow, it gets long, whether you're a boy or a girl. If you cut it short, then it's short."

"There's this picture of my dad in college with a ponytail—whoa!" Tay hooted. "Now he doesn't even have enough hair on his head to ..."

Matt glowered at Tay.

"Not this again," Quinn groaned.

"I smell a sermon coming." Neally wrinkled her nose and crossed her arms over her chest. "Let me guess, Matt: they preach about hair in your church? That must be *so* interesting."

"That's not the point. Mickey's trying to be something she's not. Boys need to be boys and girls should have to be girls. Maybe you don't like it, but it's God's law. What makes you a good person is being what you're supposed to be. But then," Matt added haughtily, "I don't expect people like *you* would understand."

"Mickey is a good person," Quinn said calmly.

"Why are you even bothering?" Neally spoke to Quinn as if they were alone. "It's like talking back to an answering machine. It's mechanical; it can't understand what you're saying."

"We got a new answering machine," Mickey said. "The message voice sounds like an old man with flappy gums."

"Nobody said Mickey's not a good person." Tay lightly cuffed Mickey's ear. "Let's get going," he pleaded to Matt.

Matt ignored Tay. "To be a *truly* good person, you can't think you can know things on your own. That's like making it up. You'd understand if you went to the right church."

"So, if I want to be a good person I'll go to your church? And if I want to be an elephant," Neally snorted, "I'll go to the zoo."

"I'd *love* to be an elephant." Mickey's eyes widened. "You could suck up water with your nose and squirt people with your elephant booger water!"

"Like any of you could even understand." Matt sneered. "Tay, we gotta go. The Scout meeting needs to start on time, 'cause I have to leave on time. We're packing for the trip tonight."

"Are you going on a Scout campout?" Mickey asked Tay. "Do sisters ever get to go along?"

"There's no Scout trip." Tay looked perplexed.

"It's just me, my family." Matt puffed out his chest.

"Our family goes on a retreat. We do it every year, and I get to miss a day of school for it."

"Oh, *that* trip," Tay said.

"Is that what your dad was talking about with Ms. Blakeman?" Neally asked. "He brought her a note this morning, before the field trip," she explained to Quinn.

"It wasn't a note, it was an advance excused absence form," Matt said proudly. "You can only get those from the principal's office. Ha-ha-ha-ha-ha, I get out of school tomorrow."

"Why do you have to leave Scouts early?" Tay asked. "We're gonna make popcorn balls after the meeting. Besides, it's not like there's a lot to pack." Tay looked at Neally and Quinn. "They just stay in a motel for a weekend and read religious stuff."

"We do other things too," Matt insisted. "We can stay up as late as we want and play games. I hold the family record for most Go Fish games won in a row. Last year I almost beat my dad at Battleship. No one beats my dad at anything."

"And no one else can come along, and they can't go outside or listen to music or watch any shows. *Man.*" Tay frowned and shook his head. "Cooped up with your family, and no TV."

Tay chortled and ducked as Matt faked a punch at his nose.

"No wonder it's called a retreat—it sounds like something to run away from," Neally said.

Matt turned his back to Neally and squatted until his face was even with Mickey's. "I don't expect these heathens to understand." He stood up and looked at Quinn and Neally as if they were something mushy stuck between his soccer cleats. "But there's still hope for you, Mickey."

Tay took a small step away from Matt and toward Mickey. "There's nothing wrong with Mickey." Tay's voice was barely above a whisper.

"Hey, when I get back, I'll get my dad to take us miniature golfing," Matt said to Tay. "Three full rounds, and pizza afterward. Dad's always in a good mood after the retreat."

"Miniature golf?" Tay's face lit up. "Dude! Maybe it could be a trip for the whole Scout troop. I wonder if you can earn a service badge for golfing?"

"*I* like miniature golfing," Mickey said wistfully.

Neally's lip curled as she watched Tay and Matt set off down the sidewalk, toward Tay's house. "I wish I was in a 747," she said.

Quinn threw his hands up in the air. "A 747?"

"Uh huh." Neally's voice was dry as sawdust. "One of those airplane barf bags would come in handy right now."

26

WHAT LIFE SMELLS LIKE

Neally helped herself to a hunk of pineapple from the platter of fruits and cheeses her father set on the kitchen table. She handed a slice of cantaloupe to Quinn, who stood in the doorway to the living room, observing his sister. Mickey sat on Neally's living room floor, crumpling newspapers into small round wads. Yin and Yang eyed Mickey intently but did not budge from their newsprint nest as the paper balls sailed past their heads.

"Your sister is nothing if not persistent," Mr. Standers said.

"If that means she forgot that I promised to help her bury a dead mouse, then I like her being persistent," Quinn said.

"I think it actually means 'stubborn.'" Neally licked her fingers. "Yummers, this is *so* positively tropical! Tell me again why we can't grow just one little pineapple plant?"

"Again, because we are *so* not living in a tropical zone." Mr. Standers mimicked his daughter. "Lucky for us, your mom's boss vacations in Hawaii every year and brings back a crate of fruit for all of her mainland minions." He bent forward and stretched his fingers toward his toes, and although he groaned with the effort, Quinn saw that Mr. Standers' fingers easily reached the floor.

"I pulled a muscle yesterday. I sure could use some help in the garden."

Quinn and Neally followed Mr. Standers out to the backyard, past the raised planting beds in the southwest corner, to a shed that was attached to the back of the garage. The shed had glass panels on its roof and sides, was as wide as an adult, and stood just a few inches taller than Neally. Quinn had never seen a greenhouse that small. Green*shack* would be a more accurate description.

Mr. Standers opened the shack's door. On the floor was a box of gardening tools, and trays of seedlings were stacked on the shelves. "They're coming along just fine." He ran his fingers through his beard. "It's been a mild winter, but we could still get some frost. It's too early to take them out. We'll just give them a bigger nursery."

"My mom grows vegetables in her garden," Quinn said. "She gets tomato plants from the store, and string beans and zucchini, but not until the summer."

Mr. Standers nodded. "We'll sow beans, squash,

lettuce, and other greens directly in the soil when it's warmer."

"Are these the jalapeños?" Neally fingered the delicate, shiny-leafed plants that sprouted in cups made from cardboard egg cartons.

"Those are red bell peppers." Mr. Standers pointed to another egg carton on a higher shelf. "Jalapeños are up here."

"We start them from seeds in the winter," Neally said to Quinn.

"I figure if I grew tomatoes and peppers in Washington I can grow 'em in Oregon," Mr. Standers said. "But alas, no pineapple for my pining Polynesian princess."

Neally ducked when her father tried to ruffle her hair. "Dad, what about this weekend? Is it a food prep or park patrol Sunday? Or is it a service Saturday instead?"

"We'll do it Sunday this week. You see, Quinn," Mr. Standers said, "Neally thought you might like to help at one of our service days."

"It's every weekend, on either a Saturday or Sunday morning," Neally said. "Two times a month we go to the County Food Bank to pack bag lunches."

"I could do that," Quinn said. "What are they for?"

"They're for the downtown shelter, for homeless families."

"That's cool. You do this every weekend?"

"Every other weekend. On the alternate weekends we pick up trash." Mr. Standers gave Neally a knowing look. "That must be why you got your particular assignment at the Noble Woods. Mrs. L'Sotho sensed that you were an experienced Garbage Retrieval Engineer."

"Yes, Dad, that's *exactly* why."

"We try to go to different parks every other weekend," Mr. Standers said. "It's a fun way to get to know them all."

"Hillsboro has so many parks, and it's not even half as big a city as Spokane," Neally said. "My favorite park is the one by Gales Creek."

"I know that place!" Quinn said. "I saw a beaver there, and an actual beaver dam."

"But we don't go to have fun. We go there," Neally cleared her throat and used her serious voice, "to do good things for all humankind." She put her hand to her mouth as if to tell a secret, but did not whisper. "Good things, schmood things: I refuse to pick up dog poop, no matter what." She leaned closer to Quinn and whispered for real. "Speaking of dog poop, have you ever seen Mr. Barker's hair?"

Quinn clapped his hand over his mouth, a second too late to stifle his guffaw. Mr. Standers looked quizzically at Neally and Quinn.

"Young lady, would you care to share that with the entire class?" Quinn intoned.

"We know you don't want us to talk mean about certain people, Dad. And we're not, we're just trying to figure things out."

"Certain people?"

"Do you know Mr. Barker, Matt's father?" Quinn asked.

"Ms. Blakeman has given me some background info. And I've done my own research about the families of the kids in class," Mr. Standers added, a little too quickly, Quinn thought.

"But you don't actually know him, do you, Dad?"

"No. I've seen him many times, but have never met him."

"Same here. This morning I got to see him up close, when he brought Matt to school. He came to class to give a note to Ms. Blakeman, and ..." Neally wiped her hand across the top of her head. "I got a good look at his hair. Absolutely mesmerizing; it was *National Geographic: Wild Apes of Sumatra* hair."

Mr. Standers chuckled. "I'm going to regret this, I know."

"Then it came to me, Dad, and now I understand: if he didn't slick his hair so tight, he'd be nicer. It pulls on his brain, *that's* why he's so mean."

"How do you know he's mean? I thought you'd never met him."

Neally raised her chin defiantly. "I've met his son."

Quinn came to Neally's defense. "You *would* think a pastor would raise his kid to be nice."

To Quinn's surprise, Mr. Standers did not contradict his daughter. "Reverend Barker keeps Matt on a short leash, from what your teacher tells me." Mr. Standers picked up a gardening trowel. "All that energy Matt has ... just think, if it were put to good use." He picked at a clump of mud stuck to the trowel. "I looked up their church on the web. The information is quite specific."

"Matt's church has a website? No way," Neally sniffed.

"Yes way," her father insisted.

"I didn't know computers were mentioned in their holy book," Neally said.

"Matt's dad has a special edition," Quinn said. "One with computers in it, and cars, and ..."

"And sports," Neally added. "You can find out what teams God wants you to root for. 'Thy ducks, they ruleth, and thy beavers drooleth.'" Neally was silenced by the look her father gave her, but Quinn howled with laughter.

"Their website goes into great detail about the church's beliefs." Mr. Standers looked down at the grass. "I was curious, so I drove by the church the other day. It's a shabby building, no bigger than your classroom, behind the QuickMart on Lincoln Avenue. Broken roof gutters and a sagging, rotting wooden entry ramp."

Mr. Standers' voice was low and cheerless. When he looked up, Quinn knew he was telling them something confidential, even if he did not swear them to secrecy. "There's an old saying: 'To understand all is to forgive all.' Let's try to keep that in mind."

Neally and Quinn donned gardening gloves and moved the seedling trays to a bench in the garage. The junior gardeners followed Mr. Standers' instructions while he went inside the house to check on Mickey. Quinn transferred buckets of compost from the compost pile into a large basin. Neally added scoops of moist, dark dirt from a barrel under the workbench, plus a smelly, murky brown liquid from a green bottle on the shelf. They used their hands to work the mixture together into what Neally said was her dad's world famous potting soil.

"Guess you two didn't get your fill of playing in the dirt today." Mr. Standers leaned against the garage's side doorway.

"We Trash Patrollers didn't get to play in the dirt," Quinn said.

"The Trail Fixers were the ones who got their hands dirty," Neally said. "Where's Mickey?"

"Can you believe she'd pass up a chance to play with fish emulsion?" Mr. Standers inhaled deeply. "Ah, the sweet smell of success."

"Fish emulsion?" Quinn warily eyed the green bottle.

Mr. Standers nodded. "It's my secret sauce."

"It's the best plant food, and it's totally organic, right, Dad? I looked it up. It's ground up fish guts. Maybe if you tell Mickey that ..."

"No, Mickey's on a mission. She's got Yin fetching newspaper balls, but Yang's still playing hard to get. Okay, once more." Mr. Standers bent forward at the waist and grabbed his ankles. "I might have to skip the run tomorrow if these old muscles don't get any looser."

"Quinn runs well, and very fast." Neally removed her gloves and picked up fistfuls of the potting soil with her bare hands. "Did you know that?" She didn't wait for her father's reply. "Neither did I, until I watched him this afternoon, after the field trip. I knew he was good at tag and other running games, but I hadn't really paid attention before. And it wasn't just fast, it was steady." Neally turned to Quinn. "It looked like you could have run for infinity. When I caught up to you, you weren't even breathing hard."

Quinn tried to hide his grin. He was embarrassed by the praise, but he wasn't going to protest. It had felt so good to run; he *had* felt as if he could run forever.

"There's lots of running in soccer. Do they have mixed teams here, both boys and girls? I was on a team in Spokane."

"But you're not now, are you?" Quinn knew what Neally was getting at. "I played soccer in second grade, and Sam and Tay and I did a basketball camp. I like to play at school, or in the summer when you can get a game going with friends whenever you feel like it. But if you join a team you have to go to practice and go to games all the time."

"I totally agree," Neally chimed in. "If you want to play some basketball or soccer, then just get a game going. But do you have to do it *every* Wednesday after school and *every* Saturday at ten-thirty? That's as bad as having to go to work every day, like an adult."

"Heaven forbid," Mr. Standers said.

"Kids today are overscheduled; I've heard Mom say so," Neally said. "Like Kelsey—we live on the same street and I never see her. You'd know if she was home." Neally put her hands over her ears. "If she's not at soccer practice then she's at Girl Scouts, horseback riding lessons, or gymnastics."

"I don't like sports enough to want to be on a team. Also, it makes people weird."

"How so?" Mr. Standers asked Quinn.

"All they care about is winning. I used to go to see Tay's games, and everyone seems like they're having fun, but then someone always gets mad and starts yelling."

Quinn waited for the usual speech adults seemed programmed to spit out when they discovered he wasn't on a soccer or baseball team, or even the swim team like his sister. Didn't he want to play the games? Build character? Learn teamwork? Collect a shelf-full of cheap plastic trophies with fake gold figures on them? Then he reminded himself that Neally's father wasn't the kind of father who went around giving the usual speeches.

"Cross-country!" Neally gasped, with a *gotcha* look in her eyes. "Dad ran cross-country, in college. I looked it up in his yearbook. Quinn would be a natural, wouldn't he, Dad?"

"I know better than to disagree with my wife's daughter," Mr. Standers said. "Especially when she's got a point. I do think you'd enjoy cross-country, Quinn."

"That's running, like on a track team, but for long distances, not sprints, right? I can do laps forever, but it gets boring."

"Longer distances, yes, but you run out in open areas, not around a track," Mr. Standers explained. "Although you're on a team, cross-country is more of an individual sport. And you don't have people yelling at you. The other participants are too busy running, and the few spectators who come out to watch would have to run along with you in order to yell at you."

Mr. Standers removed two spoons from the workbench drawer. "Now, to the task at hand. See those?" He pointed to a stack of paper pots on the top shelf of the workbench. "Add four spoonfuls of our magic soil to the paper pots ..."

Quinn listened to an explanation of the art of seedling transplanting. A wonderful aroma crept into his nostrils: potting soil, decaying magazines, the metallic tang of garden tools, musky tomato sprouts, spicy pepper plants. Individual smells blended, creating a new scent that, even with ground up fish guts, was better than the smell of fresh-cut grass. It was the fragrance of earth, the promise of growing things.

Quinn closed his eyes and inhaled. This, he decided, is what life smells like.

27
SMOKE-RING
WEATHER

Sam stood at the corner and gazed hopefully at the gray-blue sky. He unzipped his jacket and broadcast encouraging thoughts to the sunlight that lingered behind billowing clouds.

"Should we wait for Neally?"

Quinn shook his head. "I told her yesterday what time we were going to leave, and she seemed to think that was pretty funny. Fifteen minutes earlier than usual, what's the big deal?"

"She is a person of much sense. The big deal is she has fifteen more minutes to sleep in." Sam blew vapor rings into the air. "These are my dad's favorite kind of days. There's a little sun but it's still cold, so the air in your lungs is warmer than outside. First-rate smoke-ring weather."

Quinn pursed his lips and puffed out three vapor loops.

"Excellent technique, Master Andrews-Lee."

"Stick your tongue out and blow around it. That's how you get the edges," Quinn said. "My uncle Bill taught me, and he uses real smoke. After dinner he smokes cigars that smell like burnt cherries. When he's at our house, Dad makes him do it outside."

"It's early." Sam checked his watch. "There's nothing to do."

"The office will be open." Quinn hooked his thumbs around the straps of his book pack and the two boys headed to school.

"Righty-o." Sam pulled a crumpled note and three dollar bills from his jacket pocket. "I can pay up on my account. That sounds most official: *my account*. I owe the cafeteria …" He unfolded the note. "Two dollars and fifty-five cents."

"The teachers get there early every day and hang out and drink coffee in the teacher's lounge, but Ms. Blakeman usually has coffee in her classroom. Maybe we could ask her if …"

"You are transparent, Master Quinn."

"Huh?"

"That means I can see right through you."

"I *know* what it means. I just want to ask if she'll show us what she wrote up for the judges, for our service project report. She has to turn it in today—what if she forgets to put in the pictures you drew?"

"I-am-certain-she-has-done-what-needs-to-be-done." Sam's robot voice was reassuring in its clipped, mechanical way. "And-now-we-must-wait."

When they'd returned from their field trip to the Noble Woods, Ms. Blakeman informed her class she would write up their community service project report over the weekend. Reports were due Monday, and the winner would be announced later that week. Rumor had it the two sixth-grade classes would be fighting for first and second place. Mr. Danner's sixth graders spent all day Friday at Lil' Angels Preschool, painting an Oregon Trail mural around the school's front door. Ms. Seger's class had conducted a book drive the previous week, walking door-to-door through neighborhoods near the school. On Friday they sorted the books and donated them to the Hillsboro Literacy Program.

Sam checked his watch again as they neared the school. "I predict we get third place."

"I'm holding out for first," Quinn said. "Ours has the nature appeal. If Danner's and Seger's classes split some votes, we could sneak in to victory."

"I checked out the competition; we'll get second if we're lucky. Seger's will get first," Sam said. "The city librarian is one of the judges. I think Danner's class should be disqualified."

"Why?"

"My sister drove us by the preschool. 'Lil' Angels'

is a majorly geek name. Have your seen the mural Danner's class painted? The oxen pulling the covered wagon look like yaks."

"So?"

"Yaks are from Asia, not North America. Danner's class could be disqualified on technical grounds." Sam stopped at the school's front entrance. "I must resolve my massive cafeteria underpayment. We could play some four square before the first buzzer."

"I'll meet you at the courts," Quinn said. "I'm gonna check out our classroom first."

Quinn headed for the portable building that housed the two fifth-grade classes. Both classrooms were dark. He decided to hang around for a few minutes, in case Ms. Blakeman showed up. He paced in front of the ramp to the portable, occasionally batting the leaves of a scraggly rhododendron that grew in a patch of dirt along the side of the ramp.

"He's looking for you."

Although Teena's voice was faint, it still startled Quinn. He whirled around so quickly his book pack slid off his shoulders. "Ah, foof! Don't sneak up on people like that!"

Teena held her raggedy paper lunch bag in one hand and spun her hair with the other. She did not make eye contact with Quinn. "I said, he's looking for you."

"Who's looking for me?"

Teena pointed her spindly finger toward the bicycle

racks by the parking lot. "He needs you." She still would not look at Quinn. "Cold helps the swelling go down," she said to the ground. "You tell him to hold a bag of frozen peas on it."

"What are you talking about? Hey, Teena!?"

Teena drifted off toward the playground, like fluff from a dandelion carried away by a soft summer breeze. Compelled by curiosity, Quinn walked to the bicycle racks, but there was no one there, and no one nearby. He looked back toward the playground, shading his eyes against the sunlight that poked through the clouds, and saw Kelsey King and a group of students milling around on the blacktop by the main building.

"Pssst!"

Someone *was* there, skulking in the hedges behind the bike racks. The someone moved into a gap between the hedges.

"Matt?"

Matt kept his chin down and had a baseball cap pulled low across his forehead, which did little to hide the dark, angry, purple bruise around Matt's right eye.

"What happened? Are you all right?"

Matt stepped toward Quinn and pushed him in the chest.

"Looks like someone finally pushed you back." Quinn stood his ground. He was somewhat surprised by his own voice, which was level and unafraid. "Who hit you?"

"Not a whimp like you, right?" Matt pushed Quinn again, this time harder. "You don't have the guts to hit *anything*."

Matt began to push harder, thumping on Quinn's chest with his palms. Quinn raised his hands to shove Matt away. Matt ducked and butted Quinn's hands with his face.

"YEEEEEEEEEEEEEEAAAAAAAAAAAAAAAW!" Matt fell to the ground, his hands covering his face. "Help!" he yelled.

SSSSSSSSQQQQQQQQQUUUUUUURRRRRRK!
"FIGHT!"

Kelsey made a mad dash for the bicycle racks, followed by several other students, who were followed in turn by Ms. Barnes.

"What the ..." Quinn gawked at the approaching mob as Matt writhed on the ground.

"FIGHT! FIGHT! FI—*QUINN*?!" Kelsey yelped with confusion when she saw the boys.

SSSSSSSSQQQQQQQQQUUUUUUURRRRRRK!

"Not one word!" Ms. Barnes pushed past Kelsey and the other spectators. Matt whimpered as the playground supervisor's muscular forearms reached down and yanked him off the ground. "You'll live," she growled. She grabbed Matt's wrist with her left hand and Quinn's upper arm with her right. "You two can get your stories straight in Mr. Shirkner's office."

28

THE ORANGE CHAIR

This is not happening.

Quinn slumped in the plastic orange chair beside the door to Mr. Shirkner's office. The principal's office was a windowless room inside the school's main office. The school secretary looked up from her desk, and Quinn's knees began to twitch.

I'm sitting in the orange chair.

The secretary was frowning at her computer monitor and mumbling to herself. Quinn looked past the secretary, through the office window, and saw a pair of seriously green eyes staring back at him.

"What happened?" Neally mouthed.

Quinn shook his head and pointed at the secretary. The intercom buzzed. The secretary picked up her phone, listened for a moment, said, "Right away," and hung up the phone. "Don't move a muscle," she said to Quinn. She rapped her knuckles against the opaque glass window of Mr. Shirkner's door, entered his office, and shut the door behind her.

Neally snuck into the office and knelt beside the orange chair. "Quinn?" She glanced at the principal's door and lowered her voice. "Kelsey says you and Matt fought, and Matt's eye …"

"No! He already *had* a black eye. He kept pushing me for no reason and bumped his head into me." Quinn buried his face in his hands. "What's going on?"

"I believe you."

"But it's my word against his. He's in there telling Shirkner that I hit him."

The door next to the chair opened, and the secretary, Mr. Shirkner, and Matt emerged from the principal's office. Neally stood up and stared at Matt's face.

"Annie Parker usually arrives by eight forty-five." The secretary clicked her long pink fingernails against her clipboard. "Shall I have him wait outside her office?"

"I won't see no stupid nurse," Matt muttered.

"You wait with Matt, and get one of the teacher's aides to watch the phones," Mr. Shirkner said to the secretary. "If Nurse Parker isn't in by nine, bring him back here … no, belay that. She can check him out later." The principal looked sternly at the two boys. "They're not missing class time for this. If she's not here by nine, walk him to his class. Quinn? My office, please."

Neally wiggled her hand. Quinn saw that she was making the "okay" sign with her fingers.

"Excuse me, Miss …?"

"Ms. Neally Ray Standwell." Neally pointed at Quinn and Matt. "I know them."

"Were you a witness to the fight, Ms. Standwell?"

"There was no fight. Everybody knows Quinn doesn't fight."

"I asked, were *you* a witness?"

"There were no witnesses," Neally said.

"So Matt tells me. So my playground supervisor tells me. We'll see what Quinn has to say." Mr. Shirkner's face softened. "It's good of you to support your friends, Ms. Standwell, but you need to go to class."

"Okay." Neally slowly backed toward the office door, staring at Matt the entire time.

Mr. Shirkner addressed the boys. "So, what is he going to do with us, you're thinking."

The voice was a rhythmic, muffled pounding in Quinn's ears, as if Mr. Shirkner was speaking underwater. Quinn felt his chin quiver, and he concentrated on looking directly into his principal's eyes, hoping a steady gaze would be taken as a proof of innocence. He felt the skin on the back of his neck prickle when he noticed that Mr. Shirkner was not wearing his signature bow tie, nor any kind of tie, but a green plaid sweater vest over a navy blue turtleneck shirt. Was this a good or bad omen?

"I am not going to call either of your parents until after I've spoken with Quinn. But I will call them. You two are aware of the school's policy on fighting?"

Quinn swallowed hard. "I didn't fight," he mumbled.

"The one who starts it gets suspended," Matt said defiantly.

Mr. Shirkner held up his hand. "Not now; not here. You've had your say, Matt." He nodded at the secretary. "I want Matt in class in fifteen minutes. Let's not waste the morning on this. I'll get Quinn's story, then at recess I want you both *here*." He pointed to the orange chair.

Mr. Shirkner escorted Quinn into his office and shut the door. Neally backed out of the office and into the hallway, then spun around and slapped her hand to her forehead. "I forgot my lunch, and I don't have a cafeteria account! May I call my dad?" she pleaded to the secretary.

"Make it quick." The secretary tapped the phone on

the counter above her desk. She marched Matt out the main office door and down the hall, toward the nurse's office.

"Dad! I have to talk fast; it's very important," Neally gasped into the phone. "No, I'm fine, but you've got to get Mom's nursing book—the one Quinn and I were ... yes, that's it. Can you bring it to me, in class, right now? It's practically a matter of life and death."

29

NEALLY LOOKS IT UP

The frog clicker made a record number of appearances before the dismissal for recess. Ms. Blakeman said nothing about what had happened; she merely nodded and said, "Take your seat" when first Matt and then Quinn returned to class. But the whisper level made it clear that every one of her fifth graders had a theory about what had happened by the bicycle racks.

Matt was the first student out the door when Ms. Blakeman excused the class for morning recess. Quinn was one of the last to leave. He thought of asking Neally to come with him, but she stayed at her desk, intently examining whatever was in the bag her dad had brought her.

Sam was waiting for Quinn at the bottom of the ramp. "I can't do recess," Quinn said.

"Why?"

"I have to go back to the office. We have to stay there 'til … I don't know. Shirkner wants to talk with both of us before he calls our parents."

"Ah, yes, to give you a chance to get your stories

straight." Sam tapped his finger against his temple. "It's a classic interrogation technique."

The two boys walked toward the main building. "What did you tell him?" Sam asked.

"The truth. Matt's story was probably way longer."

"I know you didn't hit Matt."

"*I* know I didn't hit him. But if I didn't, who did? That's what Shirkner will be thinking."

"Maybe Matt accidentally bumped into something, and he's trying to get you in trouble because you told on him about the Noble Woods. Does Shirnker know about that? I would be happy to present my hypothesis." Sam bowed deeply. "Samuel Jefferson Washington, Elementary School Attorney, at your service."

"This isn't funny." Quinn stomped his foot. "Matt said I did it, I said I didn't. Who's Shirkner gonna believe?"

"Excellent point. You need the services of a Master Crime Scene Investigator."

Quinn and Sam stopped outside the office and peered through the window. Matt was sprawled on the orange chair.

"Brave Master Barker doesn't want to brave the playground with a black eye," Sam said.

"We're *both* supposed to be here. I'm staying outside 'til Shirkner calls us. I don't want to be around Matt until I have to."

"So, until you have to, what did you do yesterday?"

Quinn grinned at Sam, grateful for the distraction. He told Sam about how he had gone with Neally's family to Gales Creek Park, how they had picked up trash, how Neally's dad had even scooped up dog poop.

"You went to a park and picked up dog poop?" Sam cleared his throat. "The Universal Park Users Manual clearly states that people should go to parks to play, or have a picnic. Some kind of enjoyment must be involved."

"We did have a picnic. But we worked first. Neally, her mom, and I picked up trash. Her dad was the only one picking up dog poop. And he used two pairs of really thick gloves."

"A dog-poop, trash-pickup picnic." Sam shook his head. "That's my idea of a fun time."

"Me too." Quinn pretended to take Sam seriously. His day at Gales Creek Park *did* sound funny. Funnier still was figuring out a way to describe what a good time he'd had. Yes, he picked up trash at another park, but this time was different. They did it by themselves, just because it needed doing. Nobody was there to clap for them, and there was no prize involved …

"They do this every other week. A family of Canada Geese was in the creek, and a beaver paddled right past the goslings. The goose parents didn't chase the beaver. They must be friends or something. Next week I'm going with Neally's family to make lunches for a food bank. I bet you could come along. We could …" Quinn had almost forgotten where he was, until the principal tapped on the office window. Quinn felt as if an icicle had slid down his spine.

"Quinn?" Mr. Shirkner tugged at the sleeves of his shirt. "Step inside, please."

"No, wait!" Neally ran down the hallway, clutching a large book to her chest with both hands. She skidded to a stop, bracing herself against the office doorframe. "Quinn couldn't have caused Matt's black eye," she panted, "and I can prove it."

"Ha!" Matt jabbed his finger at Sam and Neally. "They're his friends," he snarled.

"Friends with *evidence*," Sam said brightly.

Quinn looked eagerly at Sam, who turned expectantly toward Neally.

The corners of Mr. Shirkner's mouth twitched upward. "Come on in."

"Whaaa ...?" Matt sputtered.

"I'll hear the so-called 'evidence.'" Mr. Shirkner shushed Matt with a sharp look. "Then Matt, if you've anything to add, you may do so."

The principal led the four students into his office and shut the door. He directed Neally and Sam to the sofa by the side of his desk, and Quinn and Matt to the two chairs in front of his desk. Mr. Shirkner sat in a leather chair behind the desk. "All right. Ms. ... Ms. Standwell, is it?"

"Please, I hope you'll call me Neally." Neally smiled sweetly. "This is my colleague, Samuel Jefferson Washington. And you've met Quinn."

"Yes, I have." Mr. Shirkner's mouth began to twitch again. "Now, what's this evidence?"

"There's no way Matt's eye could be that color if Quinn hit him, or if *anyone* hit him, just this morning. I looked it up." Neally stood up and set her book on Mr. Shirkner's desk. "This is a medical book on skin injuries, and here's the chapter on bruises." She opened the hefty volume to a bookmarked page. "These pictures show the stages a bruise goes through when it heals. See how it starts out red and puffy, then goes to black and bluish-purple, and then fades to a yellowish-green? Here's an example of the stages on a person's leg, and here," she turned the page, "are the stages of a bruise on a face."

"Where did you get this?" Mr. Shirkner asked.

"My mother's a professor at a nursing school. What did Nurse Parker say about Matt's eye?"

"Nurse Parker hasn't seen him yet." Mr. Shirkner stroked his fingers across his chin and looked across his desk at Matt. Shirkner did not protest when Sam and Quinn came over to the side of his desk and leaned over his shoulder to look at the book. Matt remained rooted to his chair, his arms folded across his chest, his heels kicking the chair's front legs.

Neally pointed at Matt's face. "His bruise is dark purple. See around the edges, how it's turning greenish? That means ..."

"It's more than a day old." Quinn traced his finger around a picture in the book. "More like two or three days old."

"Righty-o!" Sam snapped his fingers. "He had to have gotten it over the weekend."

"We saw him Thursday, after school—me and Neally *and* Tay," Quinn told Mr. Shirkner.

"Tay is Matt's friend." Neally stared earnestly at the principal. "You can ask Tay, and he'll tell you that Matt did not have a black eye on Thursday."

"And he didn't have it at the Scout meeting Thursday night, and he wasn't in school on Friday," Sam added. "He was gone all weekend. His father brought a note to class on ..."

"Yes, I know." Mr. Shirkner drummed his fingers

on the book. "All advance excused absence requests go across my desk."

The room was silent. Matt sat ramrod straight, his eyes full and glistening, his face the color of a bleak, wintery sky.

"Who hit you, Matt?" Neally's voice was quiet, but firm.

Matt's eyes dried up and spit cold blue fire at Neally. White bones shone through the skin of his knuckles as his hands gripped his chair's armrests.

"Matt and I need to speak in private. Neally, Sam, Quinn, this way, please." Mr. Shirkner walked the three out of his office and shut the door behind him. "Carol," he said to his secretary, "I need you to find Nurse Parker right now."

The secretary scurried out the door. Quinn looked up at Mr. Shirkner, realizing for the first time how tall the principal seemed when he was standing right next to you.

"Quinn, there's no need for me to call your parents. I'm sorry for any distress this caused you. You three go on with your day. You may return to class when recess is over, and I'll trust each one of you not to say anything to anyone about this."

Quinn, Sam, and Neally nodded solemnly.

Mr. Shirkner laid his massive hand on Quinn's shoulder. His touch was surprisingly gentle. "You didn't hit him, did you?"

"It was like I said, I only pushed him back after he kept pushing me. But he *wanted* me to hit him. I could tell. It was so weird. He acted mad, but it was more like he was ..." Quinn's voice trailed off and he shook his head.

"It was his father, wasn't it?"

Mr. Shirkner furrowed his brow at Neally. "What makes you think that?"

"Who else could it have been?" Neally glanced behind Mr. Shirkner, at his closed office door. "Matt wasn't with anyone else. He bragged about how his family does a retreat every year, and it's just them in a motel and they don't even leave the room."

Quinn's stomach started churning with a feeling even worse than being falsely accused. "It's sort of my fault."

"No way!" Neally gasped.

"What's your fault?" Sam asked.

"That Matt's dad hit him."

"Hold on now, we don't know who hit Matt," Mr. Shirkner cautioned.

"Tay said Matt's father was really, *really* mad when Ms. Blakeman called him after our field trip," Quinn said. "I got Matt in trouble. I'm the one who saw him and Josh graffiti the ..."

"It's not your fault." Neally placed her hand on Quinn's arm and looked up at the principal. Her voice was confident, but her eyes lacked their usual spark.

"Matt's been hurt before. I saw the marks, a few weeks ago. He had a huge bruise, here." Neally pointed at her upper arm.

"I promise, I will find out who hit Matt. In the meantime, do not speculate about this with your classmates." Mr. Shirkner placed his hands on his knees and bent down to eye level with the three friends. "And I want to tell you how proud I am of how you've handled yourselves."

30

BUT NOT ANYMORE

Although they were told to return to class, Quinn paused to watch Mr. Shirkner usher the nurse into his office. Alan Shirkner. He hangs out by the curb in the morning, yelling at parents who drop off their kids in the bus zone; he gives boring speeches; he passes out awards; he makes kids go to crisis resolution meetings. That's what principals do—that's all our principal does. That's what Quinn had thought, up until now.

"It's twelve twenty-nine, I'm a-feeling fine." Sam broke into a skip as he and Neally and Quinn approached the portable building. "The Mighty Quinn is vindicated!"

Neally gave Sam a high-five. "This calls for celebration!"

"Not exactly." Quinn glanced back at the school's office building.

"Then what, exactly?" Neally asked carefully.

"I didn't hit Matt, but I wanted to. I've wanted to for years." Quinn sighed. "But not anymore."

Three friends silently trudged up the ramp to their classroom.

31

CHEESY POODLE SANDWICHES

Ms. Blakeman's fifth graders heard the tell-tale *click-clack-click-clack* of high-heeled shoes ascending the ramp to their classroom. The school secretary delivered a note to Ms. Blakeman, and for once the teacher's glasses stayed firmly perched at the top of her nose while she read.

Matt Barker did not return to class. Each of Ms. Blakeman's students stole a glance at the office when their class marched to the cafeteria and back, but there was no sign of either Matt or the school principal.

At lunch recess, Kelsey persuaded more than half the class to join her in the gym for an all-out, wall-ball war. Quinn, Sam, Neally, and a few other students who valued their eardrums headed for the four square courts.

"Singles or doubles?" Quinn asked half-heartedly.

"It was right here. I was standing in line." Neally pointed to the boundary line of the first four square court. "Remember when Matt tripped me? I should have said something then."

Quinn remembered the incident, and how frustrated he'd felt when he realized Neally wasn't going to tell on Matt. It seemed like a lifetime ago, as if it had happened in the second grade. How could he feel so much older when so little time has passed?

"But you were right," Quinn said. "Matt would've lied. He'd have said you tripped over your own feet and that you were trying to blame him."

"No, I don't care about *that*. I should have said something when I saw his arm. I grabbed his arm when I fell, and he had this bruise, this big, sore bruise, shaped like a mini-octopus."

"Mini-octopus bruise?" Sam waved his arms. "Does not compute."

"It was shaped like tentacles, or ..." Neally wrapped her hand around her upper arms. "Or *fingers*. Oh, gross. I think I'm gonna be sick." She plopped down on the blacktop. "You know how hard you'd have to grab someone to leave marks like that?" Neally shivered and wrapped her arms around her knees.

"It doesn't have to be that hard." Teena's flat voice hovered over the end of the line, where she stood holding a four square ball. "They just hold it and squeeze, real tight, for a long time."

The gym door was pushed open so forcefully it swung all the way back on its hinges, and the thunderous clank of the door hitting the brick wall echoed across the playground. Josh and Brandon stormed out of the gym and headed for the blacktop area.

Teena dropped the ball. "Uh-oh." She fingered a wisp of her hair and ambled off toward the swings.

Although Josh and Brandon stationed themselves at the front of the four square line, they obviously had no intention of starting a game.

"Nice going, Quinn," Josh growled. "They took Matt away."

"What do you mean?" Quinn asked. "Who took him away?"

"Brandon saw it. Right?" Josh elbowed Brandon.

"Yeah, I saw it," Brandon said. "I had a hall pass for—"

"We all know what *you* had a hall pass for," Neally said.

"Was it the police?" Sam asked hopefully.

"No. They took him away in a government car."

"How do you know what a government car looks like?" Tay asked. "Did it have a siren?"

"A siren," Brandon smirked. "In your TV Cop-Land dreams."

"So, was it a cop car?" Sam persisted. "Detectives' cars aren't marked like patrol cars."

"There are ways to tell." Brandon lowered his voice,

as if he were about to reveal an undercover agent's secret code. Besides being the best speller in the class, Brandon was a famously first-rate, if not always reliable, storyteller. "Government cars have license plates with *G-O-V* below the numbers. The car had a shield painted on its doors, like a police badge, with a picture of a Statue of Liberty-type lady, only she was holding scales instead of a torch, and two kids held on to her knees. There were big letters above her head: *CPS*." Brandon raised an eyebrow and stared gravely at the circle of kids surrounding him. "It's a code."

"CPS ... Crummy Police Security?" Sam speculated.

"Crazy Purple Snotbags?" Tay offered.

"Cheesy Poodle Sandwiches!" Neally bounced on her toes.

"It might be Child Protective Services," Quinn said.

"That sounds more official," said Sam.

"Cheesy Poodle Sandwiches gets my vote," Tay said.

"How would you know about Child Protective Servings?" Josh jabbed his finger at Quinn.

"Child Protective Services." Quinn pronounced each word slowly. "My mom talks about them all the time. Her company calls them when they need help for kids."

"Yeah, kids need help when they've been ratted on." Josh glared at Quinn.

"They help kids who need ... help." Quinn remembered the promise he'd made to Mr. Shirkner. He stood as tall as he could without standing tiptoe, and looked Josh squarely in the eyes. "Sometimes, kids need to be protected."

"You're still a rat. Who's gonna protect *you* when someone sets out the rat poison?"

Neally looked at Josh with a blend of curiosity and disgust, as if he were a circus sideshow mutant with horns, a wooly chest, and three belly buttons. "You are so lucky you were born in the USA, Josh. In some countries you'd be jailed for wasting all that space between your ears."

"Geesh, Quinn." Tay kicked at the blacktop. "*I* know what those Child Services people do. They'll take him away from his home. Why'd you have to say ... whatever you said?"

"I don't get it." Quinn was so mystified by what he was hearing he forgot to be upset by the name-calling. He frowned at Josh, Brandon, and Tay. "I thought you and you, and even *you*, were his friends!?"

Tay lowered his eyes, and Brandon seemed to have a sudden urge to scratch his shin. But Josh glared defiantly at Quinn.

Quinn persisted. "Someone hurt Matt; someone's been hurting your friend. Now, maybe he can be safe. That's a good thing, right?"

"Righty-o." Sam's voice was a little too cheerful. "Let's get going before recess is over."

"The field's dry. Let's play tag," Brandon suggested.

"Not freeze tag," Josh said. "Let's do hop or spin tag."

Sam, Quinn, Neally, and Tay started to follow Brandon and Josh to the field. Josh held out his arm to block Neally and Quinn. "This is invitation-only tag. Scouts and soccer players, way. Rat finks, *no way*. This is rat-free tag."

"Unbelievable." Neally stood with her hands on her hips, her mouth twisting with disgust as she watched Josh, Brandon, and Tay jog toward the field. When they reached the center of the field, Tay turned around and motioned for Sam to join them.

Sam waved at Tay, but stayed on the blacktop. "It's okay." Sam winked at Quinn and Neally. "I happen to like rodents."

32

MY NEW DEAD FRIEND

What is she doing here?

For a moment Quinn considered walking back through the school doors. His mother never came to pick him or Mickey up from school, not unless it was the storm of the century or one of them had a dentist appointment. But there she was, standing by the bus loading zone, talking with Neally's father.

Quinn plastered a smile on his face and waved to his mother. He'd planned on telling his family at dinner about what happened with Matt. Mr. Shirkner had said there was no need to call Quinn's parents. Had the principal changed his mind?

"Hello, Quinn," Mr. Standers said. "Your mother and I were finalizing plans for a family date this weekend."

"All this time, why didn't we get around to it sooner?" Quinn's mother said to Neally's father. "Jim and I adore Neally, and we've been meaning to have your family over for dinner. I'm looking forward to meeting your wife, and

Mickey is always thrilled to
have the opportunity to be
with Neally." She placed her
hand on Quinn's shoulder.
"Here's the plan. We'll all
pile into our van and go for
a picnic at the Noble Woods.
You and Neally can give us a
tour of your class's project."

"Yeah, that'd be great.
Uh, Mom, why are you
here?"

"Nice to see you too."
Ms. Lee placed her hands
on her hips in mock
indignation.

"Have you seen my daughter?" Mr. Standers asked
Quinn.

"Neally stopped off at the office to get the book.
The one you brought to her today." Quinn felt his face
getting warm. "Thanks, thank you a *lot*, for bringing it."

"You're most welcome," Mr. Standers said. "Such an
urgent phone call, then she's cool as a cucumber and
won't tell me a thing, so I came back at lunch recess and
spoke with Ms. Blakeman, and then with Mr. Shirkner."
He tapped his finger against his forehead. "That was
some bit of thinking you and Neally pulled off this
morning."

"And Sam," Quinn added.

"And Sam. You should be proud of yourself, Quinn."

Quinn smiled shyly. "You should be proud of Neally."

"Believe me, I am." Mr. Standers turned to Ms. Lee. "Your son has quite the story for the dinner table this evening."

"So I gather." Ms. Lee's eyebrows arched, and she looked expectantly at Quinn.

"I won't spoil it." Mr. Standers' eyes danced merrily. "Suffice to say, Quinn has ..."

"Dad!" Neally ran down the sidewalk and threw herself into her father's arms.

"Hey, Mom! Hey, Quinn! Hey, Neally Neally Neally!"

Mickey skipped toward her mother, followed by her teacher, Ms. Reese.

"I hope I didn't alarm you with the phone message," Ms. Reese said, "but I thought Mickey could use a ride home. I was concerned that she might drop the jar, and ..."

"But I carried it all the way to school without dropping it," Mickey protested.

"Mickey, don't interrupt." Marion Lee smiled at her daughter's teacher. "I'm a bit confused, Ms. Reese. What jar are you talking about?"

Ms. Reese held up what appeared to be a small glass jelly jar. The jar had no label and had been scrubbed spotless, and was empty except for a small mouse. A small, dead mouse.

"She insists on holding the jar and not carrying it in her book pack," Ms. Reese said. "Mickey shared this with the class today, during our weekly show-and-tell time."

Mr. Standers stroked his beard and chuckled softly. The color drained from Quinn's mother's cheeks and settled into her throat, and she gingerly took the jar from Ms. Reese. "Mickey, where on earth did you get a dead mouse?"

"At Cole's house. He lives down the street," Mickey explained to her teacher. "He's five, so he's not in real school yet, just preschool. We found it in his basement. It's my new friend."

"That's the one you wanted me to help you bury, and you brought it to school?" Quinn gasped. "It's dead, Mickey."

"Well, *duh*." Mickey's jaw jutted up and out. "It's my new dead friend."

A small group of students had gathered around Quinn's mother. Kelsey King squeezed past Quinn and looked admiringly at the jar. "HEY, IT'S DEAD! LOOK AT ITS TEETH!"

"Cole's mom put out mousetraps, and we rescued this one," Mickey said.

"Mickey, you know better than to touch a mousetrap," Ms. Lee scolded. "You could have broken a finger, or ..."

"MY MOM CAUGHT HER FINGER IN A GOPHER TRAP WHEN WE WERE ON VACATION IN TEXAS. YOU SHOULDA HEARD WHAT SHE YELLED!"

"We probably did." Neally elbowed Quinn.

"NAH, THAT WAS LAST YEAR." Kelsey looked quizzically at Neally. "YOU WERE STILL UP IN SPOKANE."

"Like I said, we probably did," Neally said flatly.

"I am so, so sorry." Quinn's mother gingerly wrapped her hands around the jar. "I had no idea she'd brought this to class."

"Oh, this is nothing." Ms. Reese fluttered her fingers. "I've been teaching for thirty years, starting at the old schoolhouse in Groner's Corner. In my second year, one of the farm boys asked if he could bring something for show and tell. I said yes, of course, and the next day he brought in the ears, feet, and snout of a freshly butchered hog."

"Oh my," Ms. Lee gulped.

"Perspective is everything," Mr. Standers said.

"I'll keep that in mind." Ms. Lee raised the jar, as if proposing a toast. "To perspective!"

"Snout, that's the *best* word!" Mickey's eyes widened. She stood on tiptoes and tried to grab the jar from her mother. "Who wants to see a freshly dead mouse snout?"

33
SEE THE DAY

"Mom! Dad! Quinn! Come see!"

"How did it get to be past eight a.m. with me still
in my pajamas?" Mr. Andrews stood in the master
bedroom doorway and glanced back at the clock on his
dresser as Mickey scampered up and down the hallway,
rapping her knuckles on each door she passed. "Okay,
Mickey, that's enough; we're all awake now. Honey, are
you in the shower?" he called down the hallway.

"Quinn, Mickey, are you up yet?" Ms. Lee emerged
from the bathroom, already dressed for the day.
"Neally's dad asked us to let them know when we'd like
to get going." She ran her fingers through her freshly
washed hair. "Quinn, would you phone Neally after
breakfast and ask if ten o'clock is okay?"

"Sure." Quinn leaned against his bedroom doorway.
"What's up, Mickey? Did Peppy bust his wheel again?"

"Something way better—come and look!" Mickey's
parents and brother followed her into her bedroom, and

Mickey pressed her nose against the window. "I can see the day!"

Billowing clouds filled the horizon, from east to west. Backlit by the morning sun, the clouds looked as though they'd been stroked across the sky with a rose-orange watercolor brush.

"Isn't it lovely? I wish we could catch it!"

"Me too." Ms. Lee hugged her daughter and kissed the top of Quinn's head. "It's going to be the perfect day for a picnic."

34
OH, YEAH

"Wait!" Mickey unbuckled her seat belt and climbed over the seats. "'Scuse me," she said, as she stepped on Neally's mother's lap. "I forgot to brush my teeth. Is the back door open?" She did not wait for an answer, but slid the van's side door open and ran into the garage.

"Mickey loves to brush her teeth," Quinn explained to a bewildered Neally.

"This might be a good time to fill you two in," Mr. Standers said. Neally's parents sat in the second row of the van. Mr. Standers turned to look at Neally and Quinn, who were in the back row. "I phoned your folks last night, Quinn, after I'd spoken with your teacher. There's no need for Mickey to hear this, but the kids in your class will likely be talking about it."

"Is it about Matt?"

"Yes. Matt won't be returning to school for a while. He'll be attending another school while his situation is investigated."

"'His situation.'" Neally snorted to Quinn.

"Translation: that's what adults call holding back details of something they think you can't handle."

"Neally!" Ruthanne Maxwell looked at Quinn's parents although she aimed her comments at her daughter. "Sometimes I think you were born forty."

"They say that all the time," Neally whispered to Quinn. "I don't get it."

But Quinn could tell from Neally's face that she did.

"Where did they take Matt? Did he go to foster care?"

"No, Quinn," Mr. Standers said. "He's staying with relatives in Portland while the authorities conduct their investigation."

"I could tell the authorities about the bruises I saw." Neally elbowed Quinn. "It's so official, having something to tell the authorities."

"Me too," Quinn said eagerly. "I can talk to the authorities."

"Quinn had an *Oh, Yeah!* moment," Neally said. "He told me about it when he called this morning."

"An *Oh, Yeah!* moment?" Quinn's mother turned around in the front seat and looked questioningly at Neally.

"It's when you remember something that happened, and you suddenly realize it's important. But you didn't know how important when you first saw it."

"Oh, yes," Ruthanne Maxwell nodded, "*that* kind of moment."

· · · · · ·

"What was this memory, Quinn?" Mr. Standers asked.

"I was brushing my teeth last night, and I started thinking about Neally seeing bruises on Matt's arm. Matt always has scratches and bruises on his arm. He plays a lot of sports, so I figured you could get scrapes and stuff doing that."

Quinn paused, noting the warm feeling in his stomach. It felt good, in an odd way, to be the center of attention. Four adults were turned around in their seats, and along with The Girl With the Coolest Name Ever, they hung on his every word. If only his words were about something—or someone—else.

"I didn't think about it before, but some of the bruises were in places you wouldn't think they'd be. I never saw them on Tay or Josh or Kelsey, or the other kids who played sports."

"Tell them about the ..."

"I'm getting there!" Quinn snapped at Neally.

"Sorry," Neally said meekly.

Neally's parents exchanged glances, and Quinn saw the trace of a smile dance across Mr. Standers' face.

"What I remembered was some weird marks Matt had at the beginning of school. They were half scratches, half bruises. It's hard to describe; they went crossways, here." Quinn pointed to his forearm. "I asked Matt about it. He said Tay gave him an Indian burn."

"Tay gave Matt an Indian burn?" Neally asked Quinn.

"I don't think so. I asked Tay about it, when Matt wasn't around. Tay said he didn't know what I was talking about, and that I could get in trouble for making fun of Native Americans."

Quinn's mother chuckled softly. "The important thing," she said, "is that Matt is safe. As Mr. Standers said, we don't know all the details. Quinn, Neally, perhaps you two can set the example in your class, and stop others from spreading rumors."

"Great idea, Mom," Quinn said brightly. "That'll make us *real* popular."

"This is what comes from being born forty," Neally groused. "You have to set an example. We'll be social lepers."

"Never underestimate the power of a social leper." Mr. Standers flashed a wicked grin at the back seat. "I hear they get their own special section in the school yearbook."

"Yikes!" Quinn clapped his palms over his eyes. "Can we get going now?"

Quinn's father tooted three sharp blasts of the horn.

"How long does it take one eight-year-old to brush her teeth?" Neally wondered.

Quinn's parents exchanged knowing smiles and laughed.

"Did I say something funny?" Neally asked.

Mickey ran out the front door, slamming it shut behind her.

"What's she carrying?" Neally asked.

Quinn looked out his window and moaned, "Oh, great."

"Does she have to take that ratty thing wherever we go?" Ms. Lee sighed. "It's one of her stuffed animals," she explained to Neally's parents. "She thinks she can't ride in the car without it. Last week at the grocery store it left a trail of stuffing in the aisles. It's a cheetah; well, three years ago it used to resemble a cheetah. It was a birthday present from her grandfather."

"What's that wrapped around its stomach?" Ms. Maxwell asked.

"Duct tape, her latest obsession, which she wraps around everything. Don't worry," Ms. Lee reassured her husband, "I spoke to her about your toothbrush. She promised never to do it again."

Mickey climbed into the back seat. "Can you scoot next to Quinn?" she asked Neally. "I want to look out." Mickey pressed her face to the window and waved goodbye to her house. "Ow-wee!" She covered her eyes. "The sun is brighting me."

Quinn squinted and turned away from the window. "Don't worry, the clouds will come back. I hope."

"Have you met our Native Oregonians?" Ms. Lee winked at Neally's parents. "They whine about the rain and clouds, then the moment it clears up, they act like they're blinded by a sliver of sunlight. Sometimes we think we're raising vampires."

"Mickey, I love your cheetah," Neally's mother said. "I hope you'll let me pet it when we get to the park."

"The duct tape feels so soft on your hands," Quinn teased.

Mickey glared at Quinn and puffed out her lower lip.

"That's a way cool cheetah!" Neally beamed her most dazzling smile at Mickey.

"I *know* what you're doing." Mickey covered her ears. "Don't anyone be happy at me."

"Marion, Jim, we appreciate you driving," Ms. Maxwell said. "Bryan and I want to treat everyone to a post-picnic dessert. We can go downtown for ice cream floats."

Mickey perked up. "Who invented ice cream?" she asked dreamily. "I bet it was a pirate."

35

THE MOST AWESOME CLOUD YOU'LL EVER SEE

"It never looked this good before. I'm certain of it. You remember, Jim? The ponds were choked with grasses the last time we were here, and there was litter everywhere. Bravo!" Quinn's mother swept her arms left and right, clapping her hands together. "This won *third* place?! You all did a spectacular job!"

"Yeah, we got third." Quinn crouched to inspect a deer track in the dirt by the side of the trail, and heard the telltale rustling of leaves as a garter snake quickly slithered under a swordtail fern. He watched Mr. Standers show Mickey and Neally where a bobcat had buried its scat in the gravel by one of the bridge posts, and he watched his and Neally's mothers amble across the bridge. He watched a beaver that was leisurely

swimming upstream, and he watched three orange-bellied newts float in a pool of water, a pool that had contained crumpled paper and hunks of decomposing reed grass until Quinn's group had cleaned it out.

"Spectacular" was perhaps overdoing it, but as Quinn looked around the park he was truly proud to recall what his class had done. It didn't seem to matter what number a group of judges had put on their project.

Neally followed her father and Mickey across the bridge. "First and second place was a tie, can you believe that?" she said to Ms. Lee. "Oh, Quinn, show them what Sam did."

Quinn crossed the bridge and removed a piece of notebook paper from his jacket pocket. He unfolded the paper, smoothing the wrinkles against his leg. It was a comic Sam had drawn, showing the two sixth-grade teachers wrestling over a pizza while a pack of chattering monkeys cheered them on.

"That is too cute!" Quinn's mother exclaimed.

Quinn folded the paper. "Sam said I could keep it."

"I thought this year's prize was a plaque with the winners' names on it?" Ms. Maxwell said. "It was to be hung on the wall at City Hall, by the mayor's office, for a year. A big to-do, with the winning class getting to attend the ceremony."

"Yes, that's the plan," Mr. Standers replied.

"Sam said he can't draw a plaque, but he likes to draw pizzas," Quinn explained. "Besides, who'd wrestle for a plaque?"

"Ever seen Mr. Danner?" Neally grinned at the adults. "He looks like he wrestles for *lots* of pizzas—and wins every match."

Quinn gave Neally a high-five. Mickey ran up the trail, toward the meadow. Ten feet from the bridge, she dropped to her knees by the side of the trail and yelled, "Caterpillar alert!"

The four adults joined Mickey and helped her look for bugs. Quinn followed Neally back to the bridge. They stood side by side, leaned against the railing, and gazed at the creek below.

"Listen to them. Can you believe that?" Neally cocked her head. "My mom's doing her sales pitch. She's trying to get your dad to think about going to nursing school."

Quinn leaned out over the railing, craning his neck to look up the trail at his father. "I've seen that face before. It's the one grownups wear when they pretend to be interested in what someone else is saying."

"I know that face too, and your dad's not wearing it. I don't think he's pretending."

"He could go to nursing school." Quinn shrugged his shoulders. "That's cool, I guess."

"I can't wait for summer." Neally flicked her finger at a woodchip on the railing, and the chip sailed across the creek. "I'm going to an astronomy camp. We get to camp in the desert for an entire week. The instructors bring the kind of telescopes astronomers use, and we'll learn to identify stars and galaxies. Are you doing anything special this summer?"

"I don't know if it's special, but I'm going to a camp. Not the kind where you go away and sleep in a tent; it's the kind that's right in your own city. You meet every day for a week, in a classroom if it's an art or crafts camp, or outside if it's a sports camp."

"What kind of camp are you doing?"

"It's called Introduction to Cross-Country. Cross-country runners from the high schools teach it. It goes all summer, and you can sign up for more than one session if you like it."

"You'll love it," Neally enthused. "You could be a brilliant runner, I know it. I've *seen* it."

"Ah, foof. Brilliant—yeah, right."

"Yeah, *right*. This just might be your special thing. I'm serious, Quinn. Look at me."

Neally's eyes shimmered like the surface of Rock Creek, and Quinn remembered that not so long ago he was intimidated by their intensity. But that was then.

Quinn knew that he wasn't special, not by himself. He was not a top student in all subjects like Brandon, nor accomplished in one particular skill, like Sam's drawing. But when he considered what would be the conversation at the dinner table that evening, he knew that there were good things in his life.

Hillsboro, Oregon, was no place special. It wasn't the magical Olde England of the books he read for fun, where sorcery ruled the day. It wasn't bustling New York or exotic New Delhi ... it wasn't even Spokane, or Portland. But what was it Neally had said? Its skies change so often. And change, Quinn was beginning to realize, could be a very good thing.

Neally scooped up a handful of pebbles someone had piled by the bridge's rail post. She gave half the pile to Quinn, and dropped her pebbles one by one over the railing. "Let's see if we can make the most perfect water rings in the world."

Quinn dropped one pebble over the railing. He closed

his fist around the rest. "What was it like, in Spokane? I bet it was tons more interesting than Hillsboro."

"Not really."

"Do you miss it?"

"Sometimes. I miss biking out to the Spokane River with my parents, to this place with huge rocks that look like a giant's teeth that are all piled up in the riverbed. They were from a volcanic eruption thousands of years ago, I looked it up. I miss taking the bus over to Idaho, to Coeur d'Alene Lake. Logs from the old sawmills would float down the streams into the lake. You could ride the logs and pretend they were Viking warships.

"I miss my friend Divyesh and my best friend, Kate. Divyesh's family was from India, and their house smelled like spicy tomato and cream sauces. His mom would draw these beautiful, swirly patterns on my hands, with special ink that lasted for a week. Kate had a tree house in her front yard, and she loved going to the movies. She'd go to any movie you wanted to see, even if she'd already seen it three times. I *don't* miss Randall Harper. Every day at school he ate those disgusting cheese puff things for lunch, and he chewed with his mouth open so you could see his orange-stained teeth. Kate said he had a crush on me. Ga-*ROSS*."

"I don't think I could ever move to a new town," Quinn said.

"You could if you had to. It's not like it's up to the kids. If your mom or dad changed jobs, you'd have to go." Neally tossed a pebble far out into the creek. "I wasn't happy about it, when my parents told me we were moving. I looked up Hillsboro in one of our atlases. I *had* to look it up—who's heard of Hillsboro? I read about the weather and the geography. Mom said I'd like it, that I'd meet new friends and have new adventures."

"Grownups think they know everything." Quinn flashed Neally a wicked grin. "That's what some know-it-all told me."

"They do know *some* things." Neally arched her eyebrow. "Not everything, but some things. They knew I didn't want to leave Divyesh and Kate, especially Kate, even though I never said anything about it. Then one day Mom told me that in Hillsboro there was a best friend that I hadn't met yet." Neally jiggled the pebbles in her hand. "Isn't it amazing? Someone you didn't even know was telling me about you."

Quinn felt a familiar warmth ascending from his chest to his neck. He knew that in a few seconds the redness would spread to his face, and for the first time in his life he didn't care that anyone who looked at him would know that he was blushing. "Aye and always." Quinn squeezed his fist tight around the remaining pebbles in his hand.

"What's that?" Neally asked.

"Aye and Always. It's an Irish saying. It means ..." Quinn chuckled. "It means, 'Aye and always.'"

Neally began to hum a tune that sounded vaguely

familiar to Quinn, but he couldn't quite place it. Then he remembered Neally and her father, sitting in their kitchen.

"All oldies all the time." Quinn shook his head. "You and your dad have *got* to find another radio station."

"The Mighty Quinn." Neally smiled slyly.

Quinn pointed up at the sky. "Do you see that one?"

Neally continued humming.

"The big one on the left. It's the most awesome cloud you'll ever see. If you don't look soon, it'll change in a minute."

"How do you know that?" Neally asked.

"A best friend told me."

Quinn opened his fist, releasing his handful of pebbles into the creek, and the most perfect water rings in the world rippled out to infinity.

THE END

QUESTIONS TO THINK ABOUT

Ask a few of these and let the conversation begin!

1. Neally and Sam, using evidence and applying principles of logical thinking, proved Matt's accusation against Quinn to be false. Have you ever been falsely accused? How did the accusation make you feel? Were you able to prove that the accusation was false, and if so, how?

2. What does it mean to be tolerant, or to practice tolerance? How is having tolerance for a person or an idea different than respecting a person or an idea?

3. Friends and classmates often tease or play pranks and practical jokes on each other. When do such acts cross the line into cruelty or bullying?

4. Bullies often try to avoid taking responsibility for their actions by blaming their victims ("Why are you so sensitive?" "It's not serious—can't you take a joke?" "He was asking for it, he _____!"). Who is responsible for their own behavior—the bully, the victim, or some combination?

5. Some people criticize so-called "green" or "do-gooder" deeds. They say a small action like recycling makes you self-satisfied and smug, and is a distraction from dealing with wider or more difficult issues. ("I pick up aluminum cans at the park, so it doesn't matter that much if I drive two blocks to the store instead of walking or taking the bus.") What do you think?

WHAT YOU CAN DO

Here are some projects and activities to do at home and in your community

1. **Clean up your community park or playground**.
   Just like Quinn and his class did, you can volunteer to pick up trash in your community. You can even get your friends and family involved. Make sure you contact your local Parks and Recreation Department first to see if you are required to follow any guidelines or have a permit. You might even be able to get local businesses to donate money for garbage bags, gloves, and other materials.

2. **Grow your own garden.**
   Neally's family has a greenhouse where they grow many different kinds of vegetables. Growing your own fruits and vegetables is a great way to promote sustainability. Just make sure that the plants are able to survive in the zone that you live in and that you follow their needs for water and sunlight.

3. **Donate items you no longer need.**
   You can donate items like clothing, toys, books, or games that you are no longer using to local shelters and donation centers. Encourage your friends and family to look for items that they could donate as well.

find more online at
quinnresources.scarlettapress.com

ABOUT THE AUTHOR

Robyn Parnell's fiction, essays, and poems have appeared in ninety books, magazines, anthologies, and journals. Publishing credits also include her book of short fiction, *This Here and Now*, and a children's picture book, *My Closet Threw a Party*.

Parnell lives and writes in Hillsboro, Oregon (city motto: *Yeah, we're not Portland, but at least we're not Oxnard.*). She shares her life with one husband, two children, four cats, one bearded dragon, one corn snake, one ball python, one goldfish, and innumerable dust bunnies.

ABOUT THE ILLUSTRATORS

Katie and Aaron DeYoe met while studying graphic design at the Minneapolis College of Art and Design. They are both full-time graphic designers and spend their free time drawing, doodling, painting, and printing. They also enjoy riding their serendipitously matching red Schwinns around Minneapolis.